STRAIGHT SHOOTING

Old Turk Tarrington had already dropped off, it appeared. One of the breeds headed across to take charge of the old man's awkward load, calling out a friendly greeting in Sioux-Hokan as he came. Then he stopped mid-stride and yelled, "*Hey ha* behind you, *leski*!"

Longarm let his saddle drop to spin the other way while he went for his .44–40. The shotgun messenger atop the coach yelled out, "Don't do it, Turk! I told you he's the law!"

Then Longarm and Tarrington fired at the same time. Longarm's aim was true. Turk's one and only shot plowed a dusty rut in the dirt road between them and then he staggered sideways, to raise more dust as he flopped like a wet mop, graceful as a beached whale with two hundred grains of lead in his heart, dead.

TABOR EVANS

LONGARM AND THE BAD GIRLS OF RIO BLANCO

JOVE BOOKS, NEW YORK

This is a work of fiction. Names, characters, places, and incidents either are the product of the author's imagination or are used fictitiously, and any resemblance to actual persons, living or dead, business establishments, events, or locales is entirely coincidental.

LONGARM AND THE BAD GIRLS OF RIO BLANCO

A Jove Book / published by arrangement with
the author

PRINTING HISTORY
Jove edition / July 2003

For information address: The Berkley Publishing Group,
a division of Penguin Group (USA) Inc.,
375 Hudson Street, New York, New York 10014.

ISBN: 0-515-13577-1

A JOVE BOOK®
Jove Books are published by The Berkley Publishing Group,
a division of Penguin Group (USA) Inc.,
375 Hudson Street, New York, New York 10014.
JOVE and the "J" design
are trademarks belonging to Penguin Group (USA) Inc.

PRINTED IN THE UNITED STATES OF AMERICA

10 9 8 7 6 5 4 3 2 1

Chapter 1

As his boss declared, "I'm not suggesting this, dad blast your horny eyes! I'm warning you direct that any deputy of mine who'd be dumb enough to compromise his fool self with a she-male suspect is unfit for duty out of this here office!" He wasn't smiling.

Since the grouchy old fart seemed serious, Deputy U.S. Marshal Custis Long, better known as Longarm to readers of the *Rocky Mountain News* or *Illustrated Police Gazette*, sat up straighter in the battered leather chair on his side of Marshal Billy Vail's cluttered desk to honestly reply, "I never even held hands with that brassy blonde over in Ogallala and even if I had, it was the Pinkerton Railroad dicks who got to arrest her!"

He shot an injured look at the banjo clock ticking his own time away on that oak-paneled wall as he added, "That other gal in their gang was willing to turn state's evidence without one brotherly kiss on the part of this innocent child, and she wasn't all that bad, neither!"

Vail's eyes followed Longarm's glance at the clock on his wall as he grumped, "Just want to get that straight betwixt us before I send you back down the primrose path."

Chewing his unlit cigar like an old bulldog worrying a bone, Marshal Vail continued, "My old woman is fixing to cloud up and rain over me if I don't get home before my supper's cold. Suffice to say, this time we hear they're real lookers and I want you to catch the northbound night owl Burlington Combination up to Platteville, so as to save yourself a day in the saddle. At Platteville you can catch a westbound stage to Lyons and get there faster than a man can push a mount without no trail breaks. But you still have at least a week in the saddle ahead of you from Lyons to the county seat at Meeker in Rio Blanco County, see?"

Longarm said, "Not hardly. I know where the newly incorporated Rio Blanco County is. Nat Meeker got massacred there before they named a town after him. But you lost me with the part about somebody I wasn't supposed to look at. Who are we talking about?"

Vail shot another glance at the clock on his oak-paneled office wall and said, "It's all in these here onion skins I had our Henry type up for you. Suffice it to say for now that since the western slope as far as the Utah line has been cleared of Mister Lo, the poor Indian, white cattle outfits have moved in to graze all that mountain greenery the Indians were wasting on scrub ponies."

Longarm arched a brow to quietly but firmly protest, "The treaties Washington and Denver signed with the Uta Nation allowed all the water, grass and timber on top of the mineral rights reserved for our kind was Indian land forever, west of the divide to the Utah line."

Vail snorted, "Don't get your bowels in an uproar. Nobody's asking you to arrest any Indian pals. There ain't no Indians left in the Rio Blanco country for anyone to arrest. White cattle thieves, with two pretty gals on point, if they ain't *leading* 'em, have so far stolen over five hundred head and counting, all since the spring thaw!"

Longarm frowned thoughtfully and asked, "Don't they

have themselves a county sheriff to call their own over yonder?"

Vail rose behind his desk to hold a sheaf of papers out to his senior deputy as he replied, "It's all typewritten and you've plenty of time to read the complaints as you get your ass over to Rio Blanco County to dammit *do* something about 'em! I told you I had to get my own ass home unless I aimed to sleep on the sofa tonight. My old lady warned me over the breakfast table she'd found this fancy-pants French meat sauce in *The Godey's Lady's Book* and meant to serve it hot this evening!"

Longarm naturally tagged along as his boss grumped his way out to the marble halls of the federal building, locking up after them. So he was able to repeat his remark about local lawmen as the two federal peace officers headed down the marble stairs.

Vail grudgingly explained, "The cow thieves I'm sending you after made the same mistake the Tunstall-McSween Faction did with that dumb Lincoln County War down New Mexico way a few summers back. They thought they could have a private feud with Major Lawrence Murphy, who not only owned the county sheriff but held a *federal contract* to supply beef on the hoof to Fort Stanton and the nearby Mescalero Agency. You no doubt recall the big fuss the newspapers made when the Ninth Cav took sides in the midsummer showdown, tipping the balance considerable with them two Gatling guns. That's why we're sending in just one damned good U.S. deputy instead of a cavalry troop, this time."

Longarm insisted, "How could anybody be stealing Indian Agency beef in Rio Blanco County these days? The Ute wiped out that Meeker Agency on their White River Reserve and then the combined forces of the U.S. Army and Colorado Guard wiped out all the northern Ute who refused to haul ass clean out of Colorado!"

As they passed through the street entrance into the

gloaming of a Denver rush hour, Vail snorted, "Fuck the Indians. Don't *soldiers* get to eat no more? As you'll see when you read the squawk and stop pestering a man with French meat sauce on his mind, the Rio Blanco cattle spread getting hit the hardest and most often has a federal contract to supply beef, regular, to Fort Duchesne on the far side of the Utah line. Makes no sense to build a fort to keep an eye on the Mormons as well as the Indians over yonder and then depend on the *Mormons* to feed your garrison, does it?"

Spotting a cruising hansom, Vail hailed it and ran down the outside steps as he called back, "It's all in them onionskins I had our Henry typewrite. So wire us from Platteville when you're ready to push west into the high country!"

Longarm muttered something rude about French meat sauce as Billy Vail sped off in his hired hansom, leaving Longarm to his own devices with Saturday night in Denver coming on. But Billy had made mention of that Burlington night run and they were too close to payday for a man to seek other adventures with the pocket jingle he had left.

Longarm was used to hopping trains out of Denver at all hours. So he had a pretty good mental timetable memorized and knew he wouldn't have time to see if a certain young widow woman up on Sherman Street was serving fancy meat sauce that evening. He owed her some flowers, books or candy after that misunderstanding they'd had the last time she'd served him in any case. So he decided it might be best to make up with her after payday and legged it for his own hired digs on the unfashionable side of Cherry Creek, five or more furlongs from the federal building. It took his long legs and low-heeled army boots less than twenty minutes by way of the Larimer Street bridge and then west along a cinder side street.

Some of the other boarders were supping off the entry

hall as he passed by. Nobody commented, if they noticed him at all. After a lot of fussing about the board aspect of "room and board," Longarm's landlady had conceded it hardly made sense to set a place at her table for a roomer who never showed up for supper.

Going upstairs to his hired digs, Longarm lit a bed lamp against the gathering dusk to ready himself for a field mission.

The first thing that had to go was the prissy three-piece tweed suit they'd ordered him to wear on duty around the federal building since old Rutherford B. Hayes had been elected on a reform ticket and made everybody working for the government sober up and wear fucking neckties as if they meant to teach outlaws their three Rs for God's sake.

Since not even Miss Lemonade Lucy, the first lady who refused to serve hard liqour at White House banquets, would expect a lawman on a field mission across open range to fork a bronc dressed like some infernal ribbon clerk, Longarm stripped down to his long johns and socks to start over. He put on a hickory work shirt and clean but well-weathered denim jeans and jacket. Then he hauled his army stovepipes back on, knowing that fancy polish would scuff and dust to normal by the time he got to cow country. He filled his pockets with the shit he'd tossed across his bed, then strapped his Colt double-action .44–40 back around his lean hips. He carried cross-draw, as most other students of gunplay carried, in spite of the marginal edge a side-draw gave a man on foot, face to face and in no other position in a world at best uncertain.

He tucked his pocket watch in one breast pocket of his denim jacket to drape the gold-wash chain across to the double derringer riding at the other end of the same. Glad to be rid of the shoestring tie he'd been wearing on court duty that afternoon, Longarm left his shirt open with a print bandanna rolled and loosely knotted around his suntanned neck. Then he put his coffee brown Stetson back on, it's crown telescoped in the "Colorado Crush" worn north of the Arkansas divide and worn square, cavalry style, with the brim shading his eyes as it was meant to.

Having dressed himself right for a change, Longarm drew a Winchester '73 from its saddle boot lashed to the McClellan draped over the foot of his hired bed. Nobody who might not use a saddle gun for weeks at a time kept one loaded to needlessly strain its magazine's spring. So Longarm took a fresh box of S&W .44–40 from the drawer of his bedside table to slip sixteen rounds into the saddle gun's tubular magazine below its matching barrel. He knew he had extra ammunition in his saddlebags. He still distributed the other thirty-four rounds in the pockets of his jeans and jacket. A man just never knew, and like most serious riders of his era, Longarm packed a rifle and revolver that loaded the same caliber and charge.

Longarm kept his bedroll and saddlebags stocked for a sudden field mission. He still double-checked when and where he had the time and lamplight. For it sure felt silly to find out, too late, you hadn't brought along enough matches or had to wash your hands with wet sand instead of naptha soap.

It only took a few moments to make certain he was all set. Then he picked up his heavily laden army saddle, braced it against his left hip to leave his gun hand free, and locked up to clump on down and head for the nearby Burlington yards.

By this time it was fair dark out. So Longarm didn't spot the two men skulking in the shade of a cottonwood across the way and they, in turn, had trouble making him out.

"Is that him?" asked the younger gunslick as Longarm headed for the Larimer Street bridge with his back to the men sent to kill him.

His more experienced sidekick replied, "Can't tell from

this range. He's long and tall as they said but he's walking funny and nobody said nothing about Longarm walking funny, Quicksilver."

The Quicksilver Kid, as he'd recently named himself along the owlhoot trail, replied, "He ain't walking funny. He's packing a saddle on one hip. Where you suppose he means to go with that saddle at this hour?"

As he drew his .36 Navy Colt Conversion, meant to attract a mite less attention when you backshot a man in town, the more conservative Studs Bacon, as *he* was known along the owlhoot trail, snapped, "Hold your damn fire till we know who you're firing on!"

The Quicksilver Kid replied defensively, "Why should I? I've always admired Mr. Oliver Cromwell's suggestion about killing 'em all and letting the devil sort 'em out!"

Studs snorted, "Then he must have been an asshole, too. The plan is for us to ventilate the one and original Longarm and get away clean. I have been told that ain't always easy with the one and original Longarm chasing your ass. So if that long drink of water who just came out of Longarm's rooming house turns out to be another roomer, the one and original Longarm could still be inside, fixing to pop out at us like an armed and dangerous cuckoo bird! So you stay here and cover that door across the way whilst I pussyfoot after our mysterious saddle toter far as some better light to read him by!"

The Quicksilver Kid protested nobody had said anything about him taking Longarm on alone. Studs Bacon snapped, "Just tell me which way he went if he comes out before I'm back. If you hear the dulcet tones of my repeater, light out for our own rooming house, over by the stockyards. I won't be shooting anybody else but Longarm if you hear me shooting at all, and once I have, this whole end of town figures to be crawling with gents who ain't no pals of our kind!"

Then, not waiting for an answer, Studs lit out after the

man they'd seen leaving Longarm's rooming house in uncertain light.

Longarm roomed southwest of Cherry Creek because rents were lower there. Rents were lower there because they hadn't gotten around to paving the footpaths or lighting them up with streetlamps yet. So Studs had to follow the tall figure balancing that saddle on his hip far as the paved and lamplit Larimer Street bridge, where Studs broke stride to just stand there, cussing, as the man he'd been trailing passed through a pool of light that gave away the color of faded blue denim across his broad shoulders.

Legging it back to where he'd left the Quicksilver Kid in the inky shade across from Longarm's rooming house, Studs asked, "Anybody else come out whilst I've been gone?"

The Quicksilver Kid said, "Yep. Gal in a summer frock just come down them steps to greet a short cuss in a seersucker jacket. I was somehow able to resist the temptation. What about yourself?"

Studs spat and said, "Stockyard poke riding night shift, I reckon. Our finger man says Longarm wore that same tobacco tweed store-bought suit in court this afternoon. Ain't no sensible reason for a federal rider on his own time to dress up like a cowpoke to court the ladies as our Longarm is said to fancy."

The Quicksilver Kid asked, "What if he ain't courting nobody tonight? What if he turns in early for a good night's sleep with the two of us out here in the cool shades of evening like a pair of fucking owls?"

Studs shrugged and said, "We're getting paid by the hour with a fat bonus for the team as does the bastard in. The folk we're working for ain't slow. They're heeled well enough to have them other boys staked out around that widow woman's house on Capitol Hill, that orphanage where a shapely matron Longarm fancies works and six or eight other places in town he's known to frequent."

The Quicksilver Kid said, "They must really want him dead."

Studs Bacon nodded soberly to reply, "They want him dead real bad. Never cross folk with real money if you can possibly avoid it, Kid. I was too polite to ask how come, but as of now there's more money posted on Longarm's head than Frank, Jesse and Billy the Kid combined!"

Chapter 2

The Burlington night run Longarm caught was a slow combination, with the passenger section hitched as far back from the locomotive stack as they could manage. So the club car was the last car of the combination and that was where Longarm chose to ride with his McClellan under the table and a scuttle of draft atop the same.

It hardly seemed fair, seeing he'd be getting off so soon, but a handsome gal of say thirty-five was seated alone at another table and sending up smoke signals with her bedroom eyes. Longarm pretended not to notice as he lit a three-for-a-nickel cheroot and spread Henry's onionskins betwixt his beer glass and ashtray to study them.

The formal complaints only fleshed out the bones Bill Vail had lined up for Longarm already. The details were easy to make out when a man had a tolerable grasp on recent history.

Up until some mighty ill advised moves on the part of the northern Ute of western Colorado, nobody else had been grazing enough stock to matter on the well-watered but remote west slope of the Continental Divide.

The Ute were mountain folk who'd been pleased to see the *Taibo* kick the shit out of their Arapaho and Cheyenne enemies. They'd joined the Rope Thrower, Kit Carson, to whup their Navaho enemies, and in 1863 Governor Evans of what had still been Colorado Territory met with Ouray the Arrow and nine sub-chiefs of his nation to sign the Treaty of Conejos, ceding all the land east of the divide to their *Taibo* brothers. Ouray had likely taken that to mean all the land *west* of the Divide was still Indian country. The Ute ceded rights of passage and all mineral rights to white mining interests in exchange for around ten thousand dollars' worth of trade goods down and another distribution worth the same every year for future years that never came.

For the ink on the treaty was barely dry before the *Taibo* decided they'd been too generous to the shiftless redskins. They pressured the Bureau of Indian Affairs to declare the Ute a public nuisance, what with their wandering into settlements and scaring sensitive women and children with their outlandish outfits and silly grins. But when they tried to back Ouray the Arrow and his people into a reservation out of the *Taibo's* way, Ouray the Arrow turned into Ouray the reader of fine print.

Half NaDéné or Apache and half Uncompagre, as he pronounced Ute, the Arrow could read and was fluent in English and Spanish. So he took his case to the newspapers, and once he'd established he was getting fucked over by the great white father, he was smart enough to settle for 16 million acres of the fertile west slope, which was more than they'd wanted to give him, even if it was less than the Treaty of Conejos had promised.

And so things had stood, mighty tense, well into the 1870s with two Ute agencies the Ute had never asked for set up at Los Pinos in the south and on the Rio Blanco or White River to the north.

As Longarm rode north that night, the south Ute still held their land in southwest Colorado. The northern Ute had fucked up by the numbers at the White River Agency.

Longarm figured Nat Meeker, the last agent at White River, should have known better. The more tolerant Agent Danforth he replaced had been content to let the eight or nine hundred braves up his way use the agency as a trading post and occasional gathering place. But old Nathan C. Meeker had set out to run things right, without knowing a thing about any breed of Indians.

Nat Meeker had tried and failed as a poet, a novelist, a newspaper stringer and grange organizer before he'd wrangled a political appointment as an Indian agent, speaking not one word of any Indian dialect but dead certain he knew what was best for them.

Setting out to "elevate and enlighten" what he referred to as "Savage Wards" he began by moving his agency and trading post downstream to grassland the Ute thought of as hunting ground and pony pasture. He erected his new agency smack on a traditional race course the Ute had always used for big powwows and serious betting. When the outraged Chief Nicaagat or "Jack" had protested, Meeker tried to calm him down by offering to order some milk cows. And so things had gone, with the stupidly overbearing Meeker pissing the Indians off every way he could think of, until the Ute rose under other assholes and things went to hell in a hack.

Once they'd killed Meeker and all the white men at his agency, tore off through the trees with three white captive women and shot up the U.S. Army more than once, all that well-watered range along the White River was incorporated as Rio Blanco County, for white settlers to use in a more orderly fashion.

Until recent.

According to the onionskins the elk, deer and other wild critters had barely gotten used to being let alone before cattle outfits moved in to join and feed the mining outfits who hadn't waited until all the Indians were gone.

The biggest new beef baron, and hence the one bitching

the loudest, was a Newton K. Harper, who allowed his friends could call him Newt. He owned and operated the N Circle H, an easy ride upstream from the mushroom settlement of Rangely, near the Utah line.

According to his formal request for federal help, Newt Harper had amassed a little over two thousand head, including breeding stock, at the railroad stop of Bitter Creek, in the Sweetwater range up in Wyoming Territory. He and his two dozen hands had driven his new herd south from the rails and the softer South Pass range, through the just plain impossible Yampa canyonlands, to his new homestead claim and the still wide-open range of the lush White River Valley.

There was no description or further details about the owner of the N Circle H, but Longarm knew the type. Such gents had their good and bad points when it came to opening new range.

It was not a task for a sissy to drive bawling cows in great numbers over alpine passes and then hold them close enough to matter whilst you built your home spread and its neccessities from scratch in untamed recent wilderness. It took a man who didn't shilly-shally when he had to defend his herd against timber wolves, grizzlies, mountain lions and other menaces, red or white. So as he read on, Longarm figured old Newt and his riders had tried and failed to cut sign.

Newt Harper had made it through the canyonlands to the north with most of his herd intact, had no trouble from any of the earlier folk who'd built or settled closer to Rangely, and wrangled a contract to supply beef to Fort Duchesne to the west without anybody bidding against him. But as his hands rounded up some beef on the hoof for the soldiers blue, they didn't find as much beef as they figured they had out among the aspen, cottonwood and lodgepole all around. By the time they held a roundup for a tally, they seemed to be missing more. Newt Harper was afraid he'd lost five hundred head, so far, to what seemed to be a gang of at least a dozen, scouted for or led by two gals, or one gal who changed her outfit often.

The N Circle H had been hit the hardest, but other smaller outfits, including one *dairy spread* for Pete's sake, had been raided by whoever it was. After some initial finger-pointing, all the breed and trash-white *logical* suspects had managed logical alibis.

Ergo a band of infernal strangers were hiding themselves and a whole lot of stolen stock somewhere in or about Rio Blanco County.

This only sounded tough until you considered the newly incorporated county on the mostly wooded western slope had a population of mayhaps as much as a thousand, spread out across over two thousand square miles of Rocky Mountain greenery, a heap of it yet to be certainly mapped. The Yampa canyonlands to the north were more dramatic than any such terrain in the drainage basin of the White River, but not by a hell of a lot. And as Longarm had learned scouting for the army on what had seemed the wide open spaces of the High Plains to the east, you could hide whole tepee rings in an unmapped rolling prairie draw, less than a quarter mile from the beaten path.

Neither Newt Harper nor any of his hands had laid eyes on the bad girls of Rio Blanco County, so far. They'd been spotted from afar by riders for smaller outfits and in one case by a homestead woman and her kids, hanging washing on the line out back to dry. Longarm knew from sad experience how witnesses could describe the same suspect in different ways. So he wasn't ready to worry whether that gal they'd seen at some distance on a bay, gray or paint pony had been wearing a blue riding habit, blue denim jacket and jeans such as his own, or for that matter a purple ball gown. Brown hair could describe as well as blond or brunette, depending on how the light was hitting it when most of it was under a gray or black sombrero or mayhaps a Boss Model Stetson with a high crown.

Longarm folded the papers and stuffed them back in his jacket as he decided to let the local riders over in Rio Blanco County chase vague descriptions through tall timber and jagged-ass outcrops they knew better than he did. The weak link in the best laid plans of any gang of thieves was that they couldn't just *steal* shit and *hide* it. Unless they cut out the middlemen by stealing cash to begin with, as the elusive Frank and Jesse had proven time and time again, you had to *sell* anything else you stole for pocket jingle. There was just no way any owlhoot rider or his play-pretty could pay for a drink or a new dress with a cow, unless you didn't mind attracting a certain amount of attention.

His cheroot had gone out. As he relit it Longarm mused under his breath, "Don't matter where they may be holding all that beef on the hoof *inside* Rio Blanco County. Sooner or later they have to herd their ill gotten gains to *market*, and there can't be all that many ways to drive stock through the mountains all around!"

"I beg your pardon, sir. Are you addressing me?" asked the sultry gal at the nearby table, in a tone more worried than her mocking eyes suggested.

To which Longarm could only reply with a sheepish grin and a tick of his hat brim to her, "I'm sorry, ma'am. I fear I was talking to myself just now. I never started out so crazy. It's a bad habit that sneaks up on a cuss riding alone with a lot on his mind."

She sighed, said she knew the feeling, and suggested, "Why don't you share your worries with me, then, seeing we may never meet again after passing like ships in the night, and seeing my friends all say I have second sight?"

When he hesitated, she dimpled and confided, "I'm a vaudeville mind reader and a lot of my act is mumbo jumbo, of course. But one needs a certain amount of . . . I don't know, to pull it off, Mr. . . . ?"

"Long, Custis Long," he replied with a silent curse at Lady Luck, with Platteville hardly far enough ahead to get them past the opening moves of "Strangers on a Train" with mayhaps forty-five minutes left.

She demurely allowed she was known as Madame Fatima to her public or Liza Carver to her friends. So he decided he might as well be her friend as far as dammit Platteville and hauled his own chair over to her table with his scuttle of beer and the ashtray, once he'd asked and received her permit.

He'd already noticed she wasn't drinking beer. So he waved a car attendent over and sprang for a fresh planter's punch for the lady. It sure beat all what some gals chose over beer.

When she repeated her suggestion that he tell her instead of his beer scuttle what was bothering him, he was able to bring her up to speed in a few terse sentences. When you left out all the trimmings, it all boiled down to where would anybody sell a stolen cow in the middle of nowhere.

Liza said she wasn't surprised to find he was a lawman. She said she'd already noticed the tailored grips of his cross-draw. 44–40 and he hadn't struck her as a gun for hire.

She agreed with him that while hungry homesteaders or crooked small town butchers might cut out a side of beef now and again, one had to have a ready market for quantities of beef delivered in wholesale lots.

She suggested, "Wouldn't it be possible to simply, how do you put it, stake out every pass leading out of that remote mountain valley?"

He nodded but said, "Possible. Hardly practical. Such an operation would tie up at least a cavalry squadron or more deputies than we have on our payroll from here in

July to as late as October if the crooks were willing to risk losing the stock in an early blizzard up yonder. Meanwhile there's no way we can know for certain all the passes in or out of the White River Valley have been mapped. That one stockman says he drove his herd down through and across canyonlands this child had no idea you could lead a burro!"

"I'm afraid my second sight doesn't extend to livestock in rough country." She smiled, sipping at her fresh drink.

Then she frowned thoughtfully and asked, "Just a moment, Custis. Did you say this Rio Blanco County is in northwest Colorado, near the Utah line?"

When Longarm nodded, Liza asked, "Then what are you doing aboard this train? Didn't they tell you the tracks swing north*east,* not north*west,* once we get to Platteville?"

He'd been hoping their harmless game could go on a little longer. It was less fun when the gal knew for certain you'd never make a play for her. But she'd asked and he played fair, so he nodded soberly and told her, "I got to get off at Platteville, catch a mail coach west as far as Lyons on the North Saint Vrain and hope to hire ponies to pack me over the Divide by way of Cameron Pass."

He hadn't expected the vaudeville gal to blush beet red over such an innocent statement of intent, but she did. Then she stammered, "Oh, my stars and garters, this is so embarrasing!"

Longarm naturally asked, "How come, Miss Liza?"

She looked away to softly confess, "Couldn't you see I was playing you for free drinks and with any luck a sandwich? I missed my supper this evening and . . . Oh, I feel so awkward now!"

Longarm shrugged and said, "Nothing to feel awkward about, Miss Liza. Strangers on a train are always out for what they can get from one another, even if it's only conversation to kill time. I still have time to order you a sandwich and for that matter another drink before my old saddle and me get out of your way at Platteville and . . . What have I said *now,* Miss Liza?"

The sultry brunette had both hands covering her face as she sobbed, "*I'm* getting off at Platteville, to be met by . . . let's call him just a friend with a jealous disposition and a Colt .45 on each hip!"

Longarm didn't answer.

Liza said, "It's not like you think. His intentions are honorable. He owns half of Platteville, and a girl gets tired of living out of a vaudveille trunk by the time the cruel teeth of time have nibbled at her some."

Longarm nodded knowingly and said, "I never asked why you might be getting off this train with me, Miss Liza. Since anyone can see how awkward that might be, why don't we just have that sandwich while we have time and get off at Platteville from opposite ends of this fool car?"

Chapter 3

When Longarm dropped off the observation platform of the club car with his saddle at Platteville, he never even glanced up the platform to see how Madame Fatima was making out with her jealous sugar daddy. He legged it direct across the open platform and waded through tumbleweed and other stickerbrush to beeline for the nearby Burlington House next to the stage depot.

He knew he was stuck for the night, that night, because nobody wanted to drive a stage along mountain roads in the dark of the moon. But, what the hell, his expense account was paying for the hotel and throwing in a food ration of six bits a day.

He checked himself and his load in, locked his saddle and Winchester away upstairs and dropped back down to see if they still made chili con carne right in their hotel restaurant. By diving into the ham on rye so sincerely aboard their train, that hungry vaudeville gal had reminded him he'd missed his own supper.

He discovered they still had the same waitress slinging hash up in Platteville. She seemed glad to see him, too. But when he congratulated her on holding on to her job through the recent depression, she sighed like a punctured football and allowed she'd always wanted to be a ballerina when she grew up.

He told her she still had plenty of time, even though in truth he couldn't see her legs under that sort of French maid uniform they made her wear. But she wasn't more than thirty yet, and the Good Lord knew she'd spent a heap of time on those legs since she'd been likely ten or twenty pounds lighter on her feet.

He ordered one of their Manhattan steaks under chili con carne with two fried eggs on top. She warned him to save room for the wild cherry pie their Arapaho cook had just whipped up, with the western choke cherries fresh picked and tamed with brown sugar and beef tallow.

When he allowed he could always make room for wild cherry pie and their swell Arbuckle Brand coffee, she called him a goof and told him he'd be up all night with a bellyache.

Pleasingly plump brown-headed gals over twenty or more always seemed to think a man was looking for somebody to mother him. That might have been why pleasingly plump brown-headed gals of a certain age tended to spend so much time alone after work. They couldn't seem to understand most men would rather be called short than stupid, and who was about to risk showing his old organ grinder to any gal who's already intimated he was a *child*?

About the same time she ducked in the back to fill his order, a red-faced Madame Fatima or, from her expression, a worried Liza Carver, came through the archway from the hotel lobby to fluster. "Oh, there you are, Custis. I was hoping to find you here when they told me at the desk you were not in your room!"

As he rose to help her to a seat at his table, Longarm observed they had no opera house or merry-go-rounds in the dinky railroad stop. She sat down all a-fluster and confided, "I feel like such a fool! Thank heavens I never let him go all the way, but I thought we had a firm understanding and, well, a girl has feelings and . . . Oh, Custis, what am I to do?"

The brown-haired waitress came out of the kitchen with just his coffee, knowing he was a natural man, and her smile turned to a look of disappointment when she spotted another woman at his table.

But she gamely placed the Arbuckle in front of him and said his rare steak would be ready any minute.

Longarm nodded his thanks to her and told Liza Carver, "The first thing you want to do is order a more solid supper, now that you seem to have the time."

She sort of sobbed she wasn't hungry anymore.

Longarm said, "It's early yet. You'll wake up starving if you don't eat something now."

When she didn't answer, Longarm asked the waitress what they ought to feed a lady who wasn't sick but seemed upset.

The waitress suggested a Denver omelette with white toast and hot chocolate instead of black coffee if her nerves were already on edge. So Longarm allowed that was what Madame Fatima would be having.

As soon as they were alone again, Longarm soberly suggested, "Let me guess. He never met your train. After all them promises as the two of you were exploring your . . . feelings?"

She sobbed, "I don't think he lives anywhere around here. I just asked and asked some more. Nobody I've spoken to has ever heard his family name, in a one-horse town where everybody knows everyone else!"

Longarm smiled thinly and observed, "Small town folk usually know a man who owns half their town. No offense, Miss Liza, seeing you have second sight and all, but from the perspective of another no-good man who ought to be ashamed of his fool self, I fear you were fed banana oil by another no-good man who only wanted to have his wicked way with your fair white body."

She sobbed, "He almost did! I let him *touch* me, Custis, and I'm sure you know how a divorced woman kisses a man she has an understanding with!"

Longarm was too polite to sip coffee before a fellow diner had been served. So he stared wistfully at the swinging kitchen doors as he asked her, "Where do you want to go from here, Miss Liza? There'll be a midnight southbound for Denver but you won't get another northbound this side of noon, tomorrow."

The pleasantly plump brown-haired gal was headed their way with a heaping tray as Liza said, "I don't want to go back to Denver. I got stranded in Denver when our vaudeville house folded and then I let a man I'd only known a few days feed me about the oldest line in the book!"

If their waitress had heard, she said nothing as she spread their orders before them with a game little smile. Longarm wondered why he wanted to tell her he wasn't the moon calf the both of them seemed to take him for. But that wouldn't have been polite.

As she turned away, the woman seated with Longarm said, "I guess my best bet would be back to Chicago where my booking agency may advance me enough to last me till I'm on the road again, God knows older, and hopefully wiser. So you're . . . checked in for the night, Custis?"

Digging into his heroic entree with knife and fork, Longarm told her, "Had to. Can't catch my stage to Lyons this side of nine in the morning and, like I said, no opera house nor merry-go-round."

She shot him an arch look and purred, "Not even a house of ill repute, seeing you're such a no-good man, Custis?"

He washed down a cube of steak smeared with chili and egg with the black coffee he wasn't certain he should have ordered. Then he sighed and said, "Now you are commencing to be cruel to dumb animals, Miss Liza. I've been a sport about feeding you, twice, and listening to your tales of woe without laughing at you. So where does it say you have to tease me this way?"

She demurely asked, "Who said I was teasing? We're both mature, as well as passing ships in the night, and we're both stuck here in this one-horse town for an otherwise tedious night. I have enough left to see me on to Chicago whether anyone on the train buys me sandwiches or not. I have just enough to pay for my own room next door, if you're worried I'm only playing you for money, honey."

"The thought never crossed my mind," lied Longarm.

That waitress was back to ask how they were doing. When Longarm told her they didn't need anything at the moment, she went over to a far corner to play cigar store Indian with her arms folded and no expression on her vapidly pretty face.

Closer in, Liza was saying, "I know I'm shocking you. Maybe I am really out to shock a brute who will never really know how I got back at him. But he tried so hard and made so many promises for the little I let him sample and, oh, hell, Custis, how about it? Would you care to shack up with me until my train to Chicago stops here tomorrow?"

Longarm managed not to choke on his grub. He'd been half expecting her offer. He replied, poker faced, hard as that was, "I wouldn't want you to think I'm a sissy, Miss Liza. But like I said, I got an earlier coach to catch, and unless you're a light sleeper you'll have to put up with breakfast in bed alone."

She sort of flared her nostrils at him.

Longarm said, "I wouldn't want you to take me for a kiss-and-run, neither. I say this because on another such occasion the lady I had to part company with so early hurled an ashtray down the hall after me, yelling for all the other hotel guests to hear I was a heartless beast who thought I could use gals like kerchiefs and so on."

Liza sniffed. "I know how she felt. That's why I'm a divorced woman. I like to awaken late, after a night of love, and make love at least one more time before rising. Does that shock you?"

He said, "It sounds like fun. But like I said, I got that early stage to catch and there won't be another until long after you'll be on your way to Chicago, so . . ."

She cut in. "It would kill you to catch an afternoon stage after a night I can assure you you'll remember?"

Longarm said, "Won't kill me. But it sure will slow me down, and I have many a mile to cover in such time as I may have to work with. I got to hire me a pair of ponies in Lyons to push on over the Divide as I told you before aboard the train. So I'd rather get to Lyons not much later than you'll be boarding that Chicago train. Showing up late in the afternoon will mean my being stuck in Lyons for the night when I'd as soon be miles out along the trail by sundown."

She sniffed and said, "That other girl was right to hurl that ashtray at you, Custis Long! Would you really put half a day in your old saddle ahead of spending the night with *me*?"

Longarm sighed and said, "Yep. I told you I was a deputy U.S. marshal on a field mission, Miss Liza. I'd be lying if I didn't confess I want you so bad I can taste it. I'd be bragging if I warned you what I may be able to accomplish in softer saddles before I have to run for any morning stagecoach. So let's just say I'm at your service until eight-thirty if I dress sudden and run fast."

She sniffed and said, "Excuse me," then rose rather grandly and ducked out through the archway entrance to the lobby.

The witress came over to ask if everything was all right.

Longarm allowed he hoped so. There was no polite way to say he wasn't sure whether Madame Fatima had flounced out in a snit or just gone to take a piss.

Longarm saw the vaudville gal had just toyed with her own grub and asked the waitress to serve two orders of that wild cherry pie with more coffee and that hot chocolate.

He was wondering whether that had been a dumb move when Liza came back, smiling like Miss Mona Lisa for some reason.

Without sitting down, she leaned foreward to confide, "I'm checked in to room 204. Should you change your mind about seeing me off like a gentleman at noon, you'll find my door unlatched until ten at the latest. But don't you dare think you can pussyfoot in for a quickie with *this* girl's pussy! You'll find I'm a woman of some passion, as long as a man's willing to treat me right. Try to treat me like your own fist and I hope you and your own fist will be very happy together!"

Then she flounced out for sure, leaving Longarm to stare down in some dismay at all that cherry pie.

Then, seeing there was nothing smarter to do with two cherry pies, he dug in, eating slow and sipping the hot chocolate first so's he'd have coffee left for the last.

The waitress came over to smile knowingly down at him as she said, "I would have taken the lady's order back, had you asked me. Do you have the time, sir?"

Longarm consulted his pocket watch before he said, "Going on nine-fifteen, ma'am. I hope I ain't keeping you open late."

She dimpled and said, "The kitchen closes at nine but the pie was on the serving counter out back. I like to watch a man with a healthy appetite eat. So take your time and chew thoroughly unless you're . . . anxious to be upstairs by ten."

Longarm arched a questioning brow to reply, "No offense, but you sure must have sharp ears, Miss . . . ?"

"McLoughlin, Kate McLoughlin, and have you ever heard of the famous whispering gallery in Washington, D.C.?"

He asked, "That part of the capitol building where one can stand in one corner and hear what folk are saying way over on the far side?"

She nodded and pointed with her slight double chin at the far corner she'd been posing in all the time Madame Fatima had been talking dirty. When she confided she'd been listening to every word, Longarm laughed and said, "Now you know all my secrets, and I sure hope I didn't sound like a total fool, Miss Kate."

She said, "You sounded like a natural man who puts his duty before pleasure. I know the feeling. I need this job and you'd be surprised how often even a fat old cow like me has to pass on a stroll along Lover's Lane with handsome strangers passing through!"

Longarm soberly replied, "No, I wouldn't, you skinny little thing."

Then as she sat down in the chair Liza had just vacated, Longarm asked in a desperately casual voice if he might be handsome enough for her, passing through.

They were still working that out as Liza Carver entered the Western Union across from the Burlington platform to help herself to a yellow telegram form and stub pencil, lean against the counter and neatly letter:

STILL HOPING TO KEEP GAME GOING HERE PENDING YOUR ARRIVAL AT NOON **STOP** IF NOT BE ADVISED GOAL RIDING WEST ALONE OUT OF LYONS JUST AFTER NOON **STOP** WHAT IF YOU WIRE FRIENDS IN STEAMBOAT SPRINGS TO SEE IF THEY CAN MAKE RIO BLANCO FIRST QUESTION MARK

Then she sent the wire day rates at five cents a word so it would get there before midnight, and headed back to the Burlington House, hoping Longarm would join her for some down and dirty vice no other man would ever hear about. With any luck she could fuck and suck him into staying until the boys from Denver arrived. Even if she couldn't, a doomed man said to be well hung had sleeping alone beat. For there was just something about luring a man to his death that gave women of her ilk, or the likes of Judith and Delilah in the Good Book, a low-down thrill that was impossible to top!

Chapter 4

Her ten o'clock deadline came and went as the treacherous Liza lay naked atop the covers, strumming her own banjo while she made up new positions for a man who was never going to tell on her. It felt so exciting at the time to imagine a naked cock shooting raw sperm up into her bowels as she finger fucked her own front door. But she always felt so low-down and depraved afterward, unless the brute she'd given herself to that way lay moldering in his grave.

They said the famous Longarm was hung too well for the average girl's rear entrance. Liza was hoping that was true. It felt really nasty to come with a man who was hurting you with his cock. But what was keeping the big sap?

She'd *told* him she'd be waiting up here for his pleasure, and what man born of mortal woman was about to pass up a sure piece of ass from any woman who wasn't hideously deformed?

Had she overplayed her hand with that ultimatum about him having to stay with her until the boys from Denver could get there to kill him? It would certainly be swell if she could hold him for the boys that long. But now that she'd warned them Longarm might have to be headed off in the high country to the west, she was hoping he'd have decided to promise her anything to do her dirty. Could he be some sort of gallant fool who thought it was *wrong* to lie and cheat and . . . oh, Jesus, *hurt* a woman when he fucked her?

Not wanting to waste a climax, the smoldering brunette swung her bare feet to the braided rug and rose from the rumpled bedding to slip into the pongee kimono from her carpetbag and go exploring in the dark with her long dark hair undone and the kimono barely tied at the waist.

She let herself out into the dimly lit second-story hallway and moved along the runner barefoot to room 206, where they'd said Deputy Long had checked in. Smiling dirty, Liza murmured something under her breath about having to go to mountains when the mountains were too dumb to come on in for some slap and tickle.

As she approached Longarm's hired room she saw lamplight under the door. She was glad. She untied her obi to let her kimono hang wide open as she prepared for her grand entrance.

Then she heard another *woman* softly sobbing, "Oh, can't we have the lamp out if you want to do me this way, darling? I know you say you like a little meat on your bones but I'm so mortified about my big fat ass!"

Liza Carver hissed like a spitting cobra as she heard a much more familiar voice reply in an admiring tone, "Your ass ain't fat, little darling. I'll allow your hips are *ample* but, thanks to all that time you spend on your pretty little feet, you are firm as well as mighty shapely where you usually sit down!"

The woman Liza couldn't picture giggled, "I'd sure play hell sitting down right now, with all you've got in there holding me way in the middle of the air!"

Liza shut her kimono and moved away, seething with frustration and hoping Longarm was dog styling that other bitch in her bitching *cunt*! For the notion of another woman getting what she'd been lusting for was unbearble to abide, and *where* had he found a whore at this hour in a one-horse town where they rolled the walks up with the awnings at sundown?

"Just you wait, Mr. Custis Long!" Liza hissed as she ducked back into 204 and slammed the door shut behind her. Tossing her kimono to one side, the adventurous Liza dug a heroic albeit realistic India rubber dildo out of her carpetbag, inhaled it past her gag point to lubricate it with her saliva, and hunkered down on her naked haunches to take it where it had never been designed to go, moaning, "Oh, Lord, that hurts so good! But I wish it was him and wait till I tell the boys from Denver how I want them to pay him back for me, with *knives*!"

Down the hall, of course, Longarm wasn't hurting Kate McLoughlin at all as they finished old-fashioned with half his weight on his elbows. Old Kate was a divorced woman who'd met more than an occasional handsome stranger when it hadn't called for risking her job. So she never tried to hand him that shit about him being too big for her. She knew he was worldly enough to suspect women just said that to any man hung better than a twelve-year-old boy to make them feel wanted. In turn, Longarm had long since noticed that unless you took two gals to bed for comparision, all strange pussy seemed to feel about as tight, and when it didn't, it was still, by the Great Horned Spoon, *pussy,* or as some sang it around the campfire along the trail, ring dang doo.

By any name it felt just grand, at first, with most any gal a low-down man could get at. That was why they called that first flush of victory the *honey*moon. For be-twixt the time a man first slid it in sighing "Jesus H. Christ!" and the cold gray dawn when he stared down at what he was doing to marvel that it had sure become a *chore,* neither pard could imagine ever wanting to go so crazy with anybody else, and if folk didn't watch themselves when their guards were down, they could wind up stuck with mortal enemies they sincerely wanted to murder if ever they got up the nerve.

Sharing a cheroot atop the rumpled covers with the softly curved small-town waitress, Longarm felt that comfort that only comes over a man in bed with a pal who's neither an outright whore nor a guilt-ridden Holy Mary. He knew without asking that Kate liked all the ways that didn't hurt, and she didn't ask him where he'd learned some of his frisky methods to pleasure a gal. They just enjoyed the here and now of moments stolen from eternity during the dark of the moon in a rinky-dink hotel in a one-horse town. Instead of arguing with him about leaving so early in the morning, Kate woke him before four with a French lesson, and after they'd finiished right, she told him she had to slip back to her own quarters lest her neighbors gossip.

So they kissed sincere and parted friendly. Had Longarm been at all tempted to do Liza Carver dirty with an early morning visit, he'd have found she'd hopped that midnight train to Denver, vowing revenge.

Longarm lay slugabed past seven, got up early enough to enjoy a shower down the hall, and when he toted his load over to the stage depot, he found an old Mex gent peddling hot tamales from the steam chest of his pushcart. So he was feeling good by the time they'd rolled the Concord out on the road behind it's six-mule team. He handed his heavy McClellan up to the shotgun messenger, to ride up top with the other baggage. An elderly full-blood, in a rusty black suit and cavalry hat worn high-crowned, had stepped off the walk with a clumsy pair of saddlebags lashed around what looked like a bag of laundry. The old man's long gray hair hung down upbraided. What sort of resembled a twenty-dollar gold piece hanging on a red and blue ribbon was pinned to the old Indian's lapel.

Longarm asked the old man, respectfully, if he could hand the awkward load up to the shotgun messenger, seeing he was "closer." It might have sounded rude to point out he was taller than the runty old veteran.

The Indian handed his load over with a muttered "*Ohan wasichukola!*" so Longarm knew he had to be Absarokee, or Crow, as the BIA designated folk who thought of themselves as the Sparrow Hawk People. The old bird wouldn't have been wearing the Indian Wars medal given to Sioux-Hokan speaking scouts had he been Lakota, but Crow were allowed in the mountains formerly held by their favorite enemies, the Ute.

Once he'd helped the old scout store his load up top, Longarm held the coach door open for him and the old man commenced to get in. He wasn't finding it easy, the coach steps being high off the ground and the old man's legs being short, bowed and stiff. Longarm didn't offer to help him aboard. Indians could be like Mexicans when they thought you were implying they might be weak or womanly. The old man managed to get himself half-aboard with a boney brown hand clinging to a grip beside the door and the door itself, as Longarm held it steady.

Then a voice from behind Longarm demanded, "Where does that fucking Indian think he's going?"

Longarm held onto the door as he half turned to assure a burly white man wearing a leather jacket, a Carlsbad Stetson and a brace of .45 Remingtons that he didn't see any Indians fucking anybody and that the stage was bound for Lyons.

The obvious bully, who'd obviously started drinking early or never stopped the night before, blustered, "The hell you say! For I am Turk Tarrington, a terror when aroused, on my own way to Lyons, and I am not about to ride in that coach with no Indians!"

By this time the old Indian was aboard and seated to ride backward. So Longarm let go the door and swung to face the self-styled terror as he gently but firmly suggested, "In that case you'll want to ride up top with the baggage unless you can get the crew to fit you into the boot seat with 'em. Do you need any help climbing aboard or might you be more sober than you seem?"

Turk Tarrington, a terror when aroused, stared thunderghasted at Longarm as he thundered, "I don't believe this! You must be drunk as a skunk as well as a total stranger to these parts. So I'm going to say this slow and steady but only once! I am Turk Tarrington and I am on my way to Lyons aboard this coach and I don't ride with Indians and I don't take no shit off Indian loving sons of—"

Then he was staring really thunderghasted down the barrel of a .44–40 as Longarm warned, "Don't say it, Terror, lest you piss this child off serious."

The shotgun messenger swung down from his perch to assure Longarm, "He's just an asshole kid, Longarm. Let me have a word with him and save us all a heap of trouble."

Longarm didn't answer either way. The shotgun messenger grabbed Turk Tarrington's gun arm and led him around the back of the coach, saying urgent things under his breath.

Longarm climbed aboard, holding his six-gun aimed polite, to take a seat across from the old Indian and saying soothingly, "I reckon it's over. The man's just full of *minipeta*."

The Indian said, "I know him. He is *witko shika*. You say crazy mean. I know who you must be, too. All the real men of different nations call you *Wasichu Washtey* in their different tongues. You are the good American who tries to understand real people. You are the good American who has proven our kind innocent at times and proven your own kind guilty on others. I am called *Napeyluta* in my tongue. When I was a scout they paid me as Red Hand. It means the same thing. I do not ask why you took my part just now. You are *Wasichu Washtey.* But hear me. You have just a friend nobody is afraid of anymore and a very dangerous enemy!"

The jehu above them snapped the ribbons, and as the coach lurched into motion, Longarm put his six-gun away, saying, "Reckon he elected to ride up top. I heard him describe himself as a terror, but to tell the truth I wasn't quaking in my boots."

Napeyluta said, "By himself he is nothing. He knows this. That is why he was afraid to fight you back there. In Lyons he has a father, two uncles and four brothers. All of them are braver than he is and just as *witko shiko.* I don't think he was so drunk he will forget he hates us. Hear me, I am on my way to the christening of a grandchild. My daughter married one of your soldiers and now she is a black robe. They live outside of Lyons. My daughter's man still has army friends and many riders working for him. Many. I do not think the Tarringtons will come after us at the home spread of my daughter and her man. I think you should go there with me as soon as the coach gets to Lyons. It will take them some time to drink enough *minipeta* to fight anybody, and by then we can fort up with friends with more *wakan*!"

Longarm said, "That's a mighty kind offer, Napeyluta of the brave Absarokee nation. But, soon as we reach Lyons I have to forge on over the shining mountains to the western slope, where other *shiko* riders have been causing more serious trouble."

As they rolled along he explained his mission to the old scout who, having cut some sign in his own day, was able to follow the situation in Rio Blanco County as Henry and his onionskins had outlined it.

Napeyluta decided, "I think you should ride with me when we get to Lyons. Riders of my daughter's man will meet us there with a buckboard and many guns. Many.

After we get to their home spread, I will tell my daughter you stood up for me against Turk Tarrington. I think she will tell her man to give you ponies. All the ponies you need to ride on west from there. If you leave after dark, nobody else will know you are alone on the trail. After a while Turk Tarrington will pick a fight with somebody else. Maybe they will kill him. If they don't, how can he keep track of all the people he hates?"

Longarm laughed and, seeing he had to buy or hire horses *some* fool place ahead, agreed they had a deal. When they stopped halfways to change teams and let everybody stretch their legs, Turk Tarrington avoided the two of them. Longarm hadn't given a shit either way.

They went on, averaging nine miles an hour for about thirty miles of ever-more-winding post road to roll into Lyons on the brawling North Saint Vrain a little after noon.

Old Napeyluta pointed out a quartet of cowhands, one white, two breeds and a full-blood, across the way by two tethered ponies and a buckboard. Longarm climbed down first and asked the shotgun messenger to toss their baggage down. Old Turk Tarrington had already dropped off, it appeared. One of the breeds headed across to take charge of the old man's awkward load, calling out a friendly greeting in Sioux-Hokan as he came. Then he stopped mid-stride and yelled, "*Hey ha* behind you, *leski*!"

The old scout spun away from his baggage with surprising gnomelike grace as Longarm let his saddle drop to spin the other way while he went for his .44–40. The shotgun messenger atop the coach yelled out, "Don't do it, Turk! I told you he's the fucking law!"

Then Longarm and Turk Tarrington fired at the same time. Longarm's aim was true. Turk's one and only shot plowed a dusty rut in the dirt road between them and then he staggered sideways, clear of the rear of the stage he'd thrown down from, to raise more dust as he flopped like a wet mop, graceful as a beached whale with two hundred grains of lead in his heart, dead as a turd in a milk bucket.

In the ear-ringing silence that settled in, Longarm swore and let fly with, "Suffering snakes with all the trimmings, if this lucky streak ain't just too much to bear!"

The breed kid who'd called the warning moved in, declaring, "I was sure that *iktomey* was going to nail you. So what are you pissing and moaning about, *Wasichu*? You just now *won*!"

To which Longarm could only reply, "I noticed. They never sent me up this way to fight the bully of a tiny town and *now* look what the asshole just made me do!"

Chapter 5

Ned Buntline's Wild West stories to the contrary notwithsanding, it was against the law and rough on your pistol to just blow down your barrel and ride into the sunset after putting a bullet in a man in front of witnesses. But after that the local law could be pragmatic, and the late Turk Tarrington had hailed from a clan as mean and arguably more ferocious than he'd been.

Hence, with the Tarringtons hopefully still ignorant of a death in the family, and the scene of the shooting being an hour's ride from their spread to the north, the Boulder County undersheriff in charge around Lyons figured a signed deposition from a fellow lawman backed by more than one witness should hold the coroner and save him more work if Longarm just rode on over to Rio Blanco County to catch them crooks.

So Longarm and his saddle rode on the buckboard with old Napeyluta. The old scout got to ride the sprung seat with the driver as a guest of honor while Longarm rode backward behind his saddle and other shit spread across the flatbed, with his boots dangling off the rear end so's he could cover their back trail with his Winchester across his thighs.

He wasn't there, so he could only imagine the scene when a rider from town got out to the Tarrington spread to tell Turk's father, two uncles and four brothers what had happened. He was hoping he'd never know.

The scene was brighter when they busted through second-growth aspen to a grassy dell where old Napeyluta's daughter, her brawny cavalry sergeant and other adults with a whole posse of mostly breed-looking kids were waving from the dooryard of a sprawl of mostly log construction. As Longarm propped one boot heel on the wagon bed to ride in the rest of the way sideways, he could see they'd put in a heap of work on corrals and pens out back. It was too early to say whether they'd drilled in eight or ten acres of potatoes or bush beans. But the truck garden closer to the seperate kitchen shed was already providing herbs and salad greens for high summer supping out back, weather permitting. It rained more up this way than down on the plains around Denver.

Longarm, the old Indian and their baggage got off in the dooryard before the buckboard and the ponies their armed escorts had ridden were led away. Napeyluta's daughter looked to be around thirty, with enough white blood to inspire some questions, had such questions been deemed proper west of say Longitude 100°. It was easy to see why her ruggedly handsome if balding army man had been inspired to do right by a squaw. They made a handsome couple. As Longarm and Sergeant Weismann shook friendly, old Napeyluta rattled like a coffee grinder in Sioux-Hokan to Miss Pteweya, or Buffie, as she prefered to be called these days, since her Indian name translated something like Buffalo Woman. Her old man had no sooner finished when Buffie Weismann turned to her man to point at Longarm and gasp, "Wolfgang! My father says this *wasichukola* took his part in a quarrel with one of those Tarrington brothers! Then the Tarrington tried to shoot them. This *wasichukola* shot him instead. Does that mean we are at war with the Tarringtons?"

The burly former cavalry rider said, "Not if they know what's good for them. Let's all go inside and map some strategy sitting down with beer and pinyon nuts."

They did, the men of course doing all the talking as the lady of the house and other women just kept the beer, pine nuts and later some coffee and cake coming.

Sergeant Weismann agreed with Longarm's plan as the easiest on all concerned. They had cow ponies to burn out in the corral. Most were Ute or local Kimoho stock, bred to thrive on mountain greenery and fit to carry serious loads up serious mountain grades. Weismann said he was welcome to stay the night and if need be fort up with him and his boys. But he didn't argue worth spit when Longarm allowed it made more sense if he was to saddle up and ride within the hour, leading a barebacked spare to share the considerable burden of a good-sized man in an overloaded army saddle.

So they went out back, and soon had Longarm fixed up with a paint mare and a buckskin gelding that looked equally frisky. When Longarm asked what the justice department owed for such handsome mounts, the burly German-American blustered, "Do you think any man with Indian in-laws would take *mazaska* from any *kola*? Herr Gott, I'd be sleeping on the sofa for a month of Sundays if I asked payment from a man who took her daddy's part *without* having to shoot anybody!"

So they shook on it and one of their full-blood hands helped Longarm saddle the paint and harness the buckskin to a twenty-foot lead rope. Miss Buffie brought the baby they were fixing to christen out for him to admire and bawled like a baby her ownself as she blurted, "If I was not married I would thank you in a more womanly way for standing up for my poor old father! He was old and cranky when my mother had me by him because her own kind scorned her. I know he rubs you *wasichun* the wrong way with his proud silences and that silly medal he wears. But he is my father and . . ."

"He's a combat veteran of the Indian Wars, Miss Buffie." Longarm cut in, adding, "I was there, too. So, like you husband, I see no call to slight any man who fought that hard for these United States just because he's old and bowlegged."

"And Indian?" she insisted.

Longarm said, "Whatever," and forked himself into the saddle to wave his hat at everyone in sight, jerk the lead rope and head back the way they'd come, through that second-growth aspen.

Longarm mostly admired the quaking aspen tree that edged cottonwood out where the water table was a tad higher. Cottonwood roots dove deep for water, and once you had a cottonwood sapling established, you could forget about watering it, making it a favorite street tree in prairie towns. Aspen rooted shallow and, most peculiar of all, in one bunch. It set seeds like any other tree, but living in such uncertain climates, its scattered seeds had a hell of a time sprouting. So once one aspen had found a home and commenced to spread its shallow roots far and wide, it sent up clones or Siamese twins every yard or so along its spreading network, so that in the end a whole forest of aspen could be just one plant when you studied it scientific.

After that your western aspen looked a lot like the eastern birch, save for having a green tinge to its smoother immitation birch bark. Some called it the quaking Aspen because its round silver dollar–sized leaves, silver on one side and green on the other, quivered and shook in the slightest breeze, with the contrasting colors making them seem to shimmer and quiver more. Some said the aspen quivered because it had been an aspen tree they used to make a cross to crucify Christ. But Longarm had read in a travel book how that had to be a crock of shit because aspen trees didn't grow in the Holy Land.

The ones growing in the Rocky Mountains tended to be be more buggy than the evergreens they crowded out after a forest fire. So had he not been riding tense Longarm would have stuck to the wagon trace on his way through the fifteen-acre strip of huddled greenery. But when he heard hoofbeats coming at a gallop, a *heap* of hoofbeats coming at a gallop, he shortened the lead rope and got himself and both ponies off the trail and into the trees to hide behind a screen of fluttery leaves a spell. It was always easier to back a tick out of one's hide with a lit cheroot than it was to dig a bullet out.

The other riders slowed their mounts to a walk, damn them, when they came to the aspen. So Longarm overheard the nasty things they were saying about him as they rode right past him. One younger nasal voice was half sobbing and half cussing as it promised to shoot Longarm in the kneecaps, cut off his balls, chop off his head and *then* kill him!

Longarm dismounted as soon as they'd passed and tethered his stock among the birchlike trunks to brouse tasty aspen leaves while he eased through the second growth with his saddle gun. For any man who'd leave friends to fight his battles alone would fuck his mother and piss on his father's grave.

So Longarm was watching, at easy rifle range on his belly, betwixt two tree boles, as the seven riders who had to be the Tarrington clan reined in halfway down the grassy slope, their backs to Longarm and his Winchester as they faced Wolfgang Weismann and his dismounted twelve disciples. Weismann and his boys had ordered the Tarringtons to rein in at easy pistol range. So everyone had to yell loud enough for Longarm to make out as they parleyed.

A heavyset cuss in fringed buckskins Longarm figured

for the late Turk Tarrington's dear old dad was shouting, "We know he's in there, Sarge. But our feud is with him and him alone, seeing your father-in-law never asked nobody to horn in. So why don't you save you and yours a heap of trouble and just send the bastard out to us or, hell, let him cut out the back way if that's your pleasure!"

Sergeant Weismann yelled back, "Why don't you save *yourselves* a heap of trouble and get the fuck off my land! I told you he ain't here. Are you calling me a liar to my face, Buck Tarrington?"

The leader of the Tarrington clan called out, "Don't get your shit hot if there's no need to! I ain't saying he ain't still in there, I just want to see for my ownself."

Weismann said, "When I was little I wanted a white pony with wings and a puppy dog that would do my homework for me. By the time I grew up I'd learned we don't always get what we want. I told you the man you want is long gone. I told you nobody's barging past me to worry my woman and our child without a fight, and like my father-in-law likes to say, I have spoken!"

"Let's kill 'em all, Pa!" whined that same annoying brother.

But Buck Tarrington hadn't gotten that old by being stupid as well as vicious. He called out, "Do I have your word, man to man, Longarm ain't on this property, Sergeant Weismann?"

It seemed to Longarm that Weismann was looking right at him as he yelled back, "Not unless he's *hiding* somewheres on it. If he ain't, he's long gone. So you and yours have no business and sure ain't welcome on my land. So what's it going to be?"

Buck Tarrington bawled, "Our feud's with Longarm, and from what I've been told in town just now that's feud enough to wage at a time. So seeing I have your word and as long as it's understood you never made me eat no crow, I reckon me and my boys will just ride on till we cut the trail of the son of a bitch, track him down and kill him slow!"

Wolfgang Weismann suggested in a neighborly tone, "Why don't you let it go, Buck? I know your boy meant well, but he was in the wrong when he drew first and a damn fool when he drew on the man he drew on! I've heard talk and read the papers about Colorado's answer to the late Wild Bill and if I was you I'd consider the protracted existence of the kin I had left!"

Buck Tarrington's age was beginning to show through his bluster as he called back, "You ain't me, no offense, and when a Tarrington loses kin to an outsider, in the right or in the wrong, he's got a blood feud on his hands to the end of time or however long it takes to take blood revenge, see?"

The old army man replied, "I'm starting to. I've always wondered how come there's so few Tarringtons in this world next to say Smiths or Browns or even Weismanns."

As he said this Weismann waved in the general direction nobody had seen Longarm ride off toward. It wasn't a flat lie when you studied on it. But it served to inspire Buck Tarrington to declare, "Let's be on our way, then, boys. Got to cut his trail before nightfall and it ain't getting a lick earlier!"

Weismann, bless his slick hide, had known better than to wave east, with everybody knowing Longarm was on a mission to the Rio Blanco range. But his intentional slip served to send all seven surviving Tarringtons due west along the northern edge of the aspen grove Longarm was watching from. So once they were out of sight he edged back into deeper shade, got back to his feet and returned to where he'd tethered his ponies, confiding, "We're riding due south down the contour lines for a spell before we shunpike west some more across as open range as we can manage. I know it's tougher to cut sign on a traveled trail when you ain't certain which of many hoofprints might mean shit. But sooner or later them Tarrington assholes are going to figure this out and beeline to head us off somewhere such as Jimtown or Trapper's Rock where they know anybody heading over the Divide south of Long's Peak is likely to pass by."

Once he'd untethered them, he remounted the paint to ease them all through the second-growth tanglewood, observing, "I'm glad it's them and not Weismann's Indian in-laws out to cut our trail. For I learned from Indians when I first got out here after the war that it's a lot easier to figure out where something or somebody is *headed* and just head 'em off than it is to sniff around for any farts they've left lingering, as if you were a fool bloodhound with a good nose and a limited imagination!"

As they broke out of the aspen to cross more open range, Longarm saw that the shadows of freestanding trees were getting ominously long. For what with one fool thing and another the day wasn't getting any younger. So when they came upon a narrow but well-beaten pony trail, headed to meet the low sun in the west, Longarm swung on to it and declared, "Change of plans, ponies. It's later than I figured and we don't want to flounder through strange mountain scenery in the dark of the moon. So what say we tear ass west along this trail and put a good distance in with nobody watching and one pony track looking much like any other in the dark?"

Suiting actions to his words, Longarm rode west toward the impending sundown, meeting nary a soul until just around sundown, in the tricky light of gloaming, when he encountered first a barking sheepdog, then an Indian file of merino sheep and, as he moved off the trail to let them pass, another barking dog and a wary looking old sheepherder of the Mex persuasion. Knowing how nervous he was making the older man as he sat there on a cow pony, Longarm nodded polite and called out, "*Buen-tardes, amigo mío. ¿A 'onde va?*"

The older man replied in better Spanish that he was on his way down to Lyons to treat his small herd to their first shearing of the summer.

So they parted friendly and Longarm rode on, consulting his fuzzy mental map of country he'd ridden a spell back for a good place to camp.

He could only hope that old Mex on his way to Lyons didn't know the Tarringtons well enough to talk to.

Chapter 6

Longarm called a halt after dark amid a natural saucer of granite outcrops he recalled from a less lonely ride up that way with a Kimoho gal who'd chosen it as a place they wouldn't be disturbed. He'd lashed a gunny of oats and a water bag packing sixteen pounds more to his old army saddle back at the Weismann spread. General George B. McClellan, not much for fighting but a hell of a quartermaster, had designed the army saddle named after him, basing it on a Hungarian cavalry saddle he'd admired as a military attaché in Vienna Town one time, with lots of strong brass fittings handy for hanging extra shit on. Longarm of course watered the ponies before he put the dry oats in their wet feed bags to beef up the green grass and leaves they'd been browsing along the trail during trail breaks. They were used to the country and less likely to bloat than if he'd had prairie stock to worry about.

Once he had his horseflesh watered, fed and tethered bareback to nibble aspen twigs and bark as was their wont, their species being light sleepers who fretted their way through the night on their feet, asleep or awake, Longarm spread his bedroll in the hollow love nest he and that Kimoho gal, Miss Calling Dove, had shared. As he sat atop the tarp, inhaling cold pork and beans washed down by tomato preserves from his saddlebags, Longarm wistfully wondered whatever might have become of the pretty little thing. Kimoho, like all too many other wandersome hunting and food gathering nations, had never cottoned to moderation in their eating habits.

They et with as much delicacy as half-starved wolverines.

That was likely because they'd starved some in those shining times they liked to say they'd lost to modern progress. Depending on their wits and the fickle bounty of nature for every meal they might or might not eat come suppertime, they'd evolved, as Professor Darwin put it, to just soldier on with empty guts when the hunting was poor or stuff their fool selves to "Let's puke so's we can eat some more!" when the hunting was good or the critters had left an acre or more of camus bulbs or bitterroot to be gathered. So the notion of *moderation* just never crossed the Kimoho mind, and whenever or wherever food was to be found, a Kimoho damn well *et* it until it was damn well *gone*!

Longarm could only hope Miss Calling Dove had been paying him *some* attention as he'd explained all that to her in that very love nest. For she'd been awfully pretty but mighty well padded next to most Indian or other gals, and she'd et every bean he'd had in his saddlebags.

Considering the fleshy charms of a mighty warm-matured Kimoho gal was not a comfortable way to settle down so early after dark on firm bedding. He knew better than to light a smoke for dessert. For nobody would be able to make out the glow if he lit up down in this natural bowl, but the smell of tobacco could drift for miles at night through moist woodland, even if you didn't have more than half a dozen pissed off Tarringtons trailing you.

He lay back atop the tarp with his duds on, after rolling up his gunbelt to tuck in his inverted Stetson with other lumpy shit. He stared up at the starry little patch of open sky he could make out from down here in this granite soup bowl, wondering how come they had so many such formations in the front range. The famous Trappers Rock over toward Jimtown was only an outstanding example of the odd sort of natural forts scattered along the aspen belt of the aptly named Rocky Mountains. Longarm had asked more than one more-educated landscape painter how they'd gotten there. They weren't volcanic. Granite formed deep underground in big potato-shaped formations that only got exposed to the wind and the stars after millions of years had eroded their softer surroundings away. A landscape-painting blonde who'd once posed for Longarm in the nude had said most granite outcrops started as big old elephant gray domes and later on sort of popped like big old blisters to form these big shallow saucers with rims of gray boulders strung like Hawaiian leis on deep-down necklace strings. The Indians found them puzzling and hence likely medicine as well. Some such sites were considered sacred, whilst others were haunted by spirit bears or worse and best to be avoided. That famous stand those mountain men had made against Arapaho over to Trappers Rock had been helped a heap by Indian tales of terror, as well as those Spencer repeaters the mountain men had brought along to terrify Indians.

Wishing on a shooting star up yonder, Longarm lectured himself on the little really known about the complexicated rocky ridges running from Alaska down to Central America under many a name for the same odd notion of Dame Nature.

Folk who pictured the Rockies from landscape painting or postcards, without going up in 'em, tended to imagine a sort of dotted line or backbone of snow-covered peaks running north and south. But that was not what had happened when something awsome had happened, way back when. This chestnut-headed little thing who'd studied Geology before she'd met Longarm had assured him all this high country had started out low, under swamps and shallow seas, to form thick beds of sandstone, shale, coal, limestone and such, with coral reefs and lava flows to complexicate hell out of things even before hell busted loose down below to shove most everything skyward, all rumpled and crumpled, before it got whittled by wind and water for millions of years. So the so-called Continental Divide was just a wandersome, somewhat higher ridge that snaked hundred of miles east or west as it wound its way the length of the continent and some said down into South America to turn into those Andes. Other ridges, some higher in spots but mostly a tad lower, branched off willy-nilly or rose all alone to encircle the valleys, broad and narrow, draining sooner or later into the Gulf of Mexico or Pacific around either end of the Sierra-Nevada-Cascade ranges to the west. The big old "Park," as they called the broader bottomlands making up most of Rio Blanco County, ran east to west at right angles to the main divide, draining into the bigger Green River lowlands down the mainstream of the White or Blanco River, winding all over but trending generally west. With the town of Rangely and the more settled Green River Mormon country downstream, those bad girls of Rio Blanco County were most likely running all that stolen beef north or south over the Roan Plateau to the hungry miners around Grand Junction or back north through . . . Hold on, there was a white-water river running nigh due south to join the Yampa before it *got* to those tough canyonlands. They called it the Little Snake. It ran down out of the Sweetwater country where the unhappy Newt Harper said he'd amassed all those cows. Longarm made a mental note to ask the new cattle baron how come he'd driven his herd south the hard way. What if he was a big fibber? What if a man who'd wrangled a beef contract he couldn't deliver on had just made up a tale about the beef being stolen from him and . . . then what? Where was the fun or profit in that devious plot?

That was the trouble with devious plots, as soon as you got to study on them. It was *possible* Queen Elizabeth had never married up because she'd been born a boy. But the notion fell apart as soon as you asked how come King Henry lost interest in his first two wives for presenting him with daughters. Miss Anne Boleyn could have hung on to her man and likely her head had her newborn Lizzy had a little dick to wave in old King Henry's face. So *possible* offered shifting sands to build a case on. It was tough enough to catch crooks when you stuck to *most likely*!

Dying for a smoke, Longarm told the stars above, "Let's start with the mining camps along the Gunnison, first. Makes more sense than a drive back to the Sweetwater range, where beef is *cheaper*."

Longarm had already dismissed an eastbound drive up the ever more rugged drainage of the White River forks over a limited number of the higher passes above Timberline, where moving livestock could be and would be detectable from miles in all directions. The more he studied on it the more he liked the notion of secret slaughter houses in the mushroom towns of Rifle on the Colorado, Austin on the Gunnison or Grand Junction, where said rivers ran together.

Running such possibles around in circles was almost as sleepy-eyed as jumping sheep over mental fences. So Longarm had unwound enough to pull the tarp over himself and doze some before, sure enough, it got to raining as the summer sky above cooled off.

He might have slept more fitfully had he been a fly on the wall of the Elkhorn Saloon in Lyons that rainy evening.

Shadow Vance was a gray little man who looked like his nickname and lived by his wits, having no other marketable skills or talents. He'd been looking all over for big Buck Tarrington before he caught up with him in the Elkhorn, trail weary and trying to get over it at a corner table with a scuttle of beer, scrambled eggs and home fries.

Shadow Vance sidled up to the table and asked if he had Buck's permit to sit down with him.

Tarrington shook his head and said, "Not hardly. I'm particular who sets down with me. What are you selling tonight? I hope it's a better offer than your ugly mother."

Shadow said, "I got more friends in these parts than certain big shots who throw their weight around. So a certain humble sheepherder who's scared shitless of you and your boys told somebody as drinks with me something you might want to know."

"Why should I want to know about fucking sheep?" growled the burly cattleman, adding, "Unlike yourself I've never had to stoop to fucking sheep when my momma had the rag on."

Shadow said, "Suit yourself. But they told me you were anxious to cut the trail of that famous lawman your boy tangled with, earlier."

Buck Tarrington rose, then rose some more as he quietly but firmly stated, "If you know shit about where Longarm went, just spit it out and cut this shit about sheepherders, you little shit."

Shadow smiled and said, "I figured you'd be willing to buy a pal a drink if he came your way with such information."

Buck Tarrington wrapped a jovial arm around Shadow's shoulders as he suggested, "Let's talk about it in the back room."

Then they went into the back room whether Shadow had planned on it or not. For the soles of his boots barely brushed the floor as Buck literally swept him off his feet, stiff-armed the door to the back with his free hand and threw the smaller man across the room before he slammed the door shut after them, drew his six-gun and purred in a tone as cold as the keel of a viking ship, "Don't fuck with me, little boy. I got a boy of my own growing colder by the minute over to the undertaker's. We're fixing to hold Turk's funeral after we kill the son of a bitch as killed him. They'll hold your funeral sooner if you don't quit fucking with me, Shadow!"

Shadow Vance gleeped, "I ain't fucking with you, Buck! Old Hernando Lopez told this Mex gal I know he met up with a tall Anglo answering her description of the man who shot your boy this afternoon! The old sheepherder met up with him on the South Fork Trail late in the day, riding a paint and leading a buckskin west toward the Divide. Lopez figured he was headed for either Sawtooth Pass or Cameron's if he's headed for the Rio Blanco range like everybody says!"

Buck Tarrington holstered his six-gun and broke out his wallet as he growled, "Welcome back amidst the living."

Then he handed over a twenty-dollar silver certificate as he added, "It ain't that I'm tight, Shadow. I just don't cotton to being fucked with."

Grinning down at the windfall in his grasp, Shadow asked, "Which pass do you reckon he's headed over, Buck?"

The experienced high country rider shrugged and said, "It don't matter. There's way more than one trail he can follow most of the way, but I know the shortest way to where all trails bottleneck and so that's where me and my boys will beeline to head him off!"

And as if to prove low-down minds sought their own channels, two others were plotting Longarm's demise on the far side of the Divide, in the dinky trail town of Hot Sulphur Springs, distinguished by the steaming pools that smelled like kitchen matches and drained into the watershed of the upper Colorado, near the only telegraph office for a day's ride in any direction.

They were known professionally as the Tracy Twins. They were not at all related and didn't look anything like one another. Neither looked all that Irish because neither was. They thought this was clever as all get-out because their profession was cold-blooded murder and it gave them an edge when a prospective target was on the prod for lookalike twins instead of the tall, thin Pat and the short, squat Mike.

After that they both wore sober black suits over their boots and shoulder holstered .38–30 Detective Specials for close and dirty work in town. Their saddle guns were high-powered Springfield .45–70s that fired slower but had Longarm's Winchester .44–40 outranged. The Tracy Twins had never been known to give a sucker an even break.

Thanks to the treacherous Liza Carver, the Tracy Twins had been wired to intercept Longarm on his way to Rio Blanco County. More than one traditional Indian trail passed through Hot Sulphur Springs, which was why they'd been posted there to begin with. But another wire late that afternoon had alerted them to the fact that Longarm might want to cross the Divide sneaky and shunpike his way through the tanglewoods as far as he could.

So the tall, cadaverous Pat got out their Land Management survey map and spread it across the one table in the cabin they'd hired near the telegraph office.

Tracing with his trigger finger, Pat told the runty Mike, "You can see how the Divide to the east forms a swamping horseshoe around this watershed, with a fucking pass every fucking twenty miles or less. But it don't matter, this far east. No matter whether he comes west north of here or south of here, all the trails he might follow meet this side of Glenwood Springs, see?"

Mike said, "Sure. I got eyes and I ain't stupid. If I

meant to ride to Rio Blanco County, I'd ride west along the Colorado from Glenwood Springs to the town of Rifle, where I'd follow the Meeker Trail north along the Grand Hogback to the county seat a hard day's ride to the other side of the White River Plateau."

Pat began to fold the map as he snorted, "You may have eyes. But you're still stupid. Where in the U.S. Constitution does it say we got to worry about where Longarm may be riding west of Glenwood Springs? Don't matter where he is right now, we got better than a day's ride lead on him. So it'll be duck soup simple to get to Glenwood Springs way ahead of him, shop about for a window overlooking the river trail and earn ourselves some easy money and a hell of a rep as the ones who shot the one and original Longarm!"

Chapter 7

Longarm rode into the little there was of Hot Sulphur Springs two days after the Tracy Twins had ridden west to head him off at Glenwood Springs. He was traveling light and using the same Land Management survey map printed in Washington. There wasn't much on paper where there were no traditional trails or recently established white settlements west of the Divide or north of the San Juans. But he was able to travel light by following a dotted line of settlements seldom a full day's ride apart.

Having had a couple of nights at higher altitude to consider that old sheepherder he'd brushed by, and having failed to find anybody with horseflesh worth riding at Grand Lake, Longarm took note of the corral out back of the one livery where he could water and feed his paint and the buckskin. When he told the old horse trader cum livery man those bigger bay mounts looked like army vets, the old-timer told him, "That's on account they are. I got a price on 'em off Fort Fred Steele after they'd been run into the ground chasing Utes out of the state. Remount officer condemned nigh two dozen head, all told. So I got 'em at dog food prices and look at 'em now, after plenty of rest and standing in hot sulphur water to soak the hurt out of their poor legs. I just sold a pair the other day to a couple of other strangers in town. I treated 'em right. Let 'em trade in the cow ponies they'd rid over the Divide as twenty dollars' credit and I admitted to them as I'm admitting to you those old army mounts ain't worth as much today as the remount service paid for them in the sweet by-and-by."

Longarm said, "I'm offering twenty bucks a head and throwing in these two cow ponies."

The old-timer said, "Surely you jest. I wouldn't take less than sixty dollars a piece for part-thoroughbreds for Gawd's sake! That's what I charged them other strangers the other day."

Longarm said, "They must have been furriners, then. Twenty-five a head and that's my last offer."

They settled on thirty, shook on it, and Longarm said he'd come back to saddle one army bay and lead another as soon as he picked up some trail supplies and treated himself to a set-down meal somebody had *cooked* for a change.

The cheap but strong black coffee he washed his venison smothered in wild onions down with inspired him to push on, mostly downslope now, sincerely hoping that if that old Mex had made mention in Lyons of paint or buckskin ponies, nobody would think to ask too much about it, or if anyone had changed mounts in recent memory.

Asking the old horse trader not to say where he might have come by the paint and buckskin would have been discreet as posting a sign to read, "HE WENT THATAWAY ON A BAY!"

As he followed a traditional Ute trail along the upper Colorado, hardly more than a brawling white-water torrent this far upstream, Longarm decided the old-timer back in Hot Sulphur Springs had been that almost mythical breed known as honest horse traders. For both the army bay mares he'd changed to proved willing and able to pack him and his light load at a mile-eating cavalry pace, trotting some, walking some, and never mind about his balls. Old soldiers hated to ride at a mile-eating trot as much as anybody else. But they knew a mount ridden so would carry you farther, sooner, than at other gaits. General McClellan had chosen that Hungarian notion with a split seat to cool the horse's spine, not to snuggle your balls down into. The trick was to stand in the stirrups most of the ways and let the ball-busting bounces occur for the most part in thin air betwixt your wide-spread thighs, like a whore fucking ghosts.

He rode downstream an hour, dismounted to switch his saddle and bridle to the bay he'd been leading, and let them both graze on some trailside sedge and wild onion for as long as it took him to rest his saddle-sore legs sitting down in the same. Whilst he was at it he helped himself to some wild onions as well. They tasted different when you et 'em raw, but better than store-bought scallions either way. Professors who studied botany said the wild onions of the high country were closer to scallions or those onions the Welsh mining men called leeks. But Colorado riders called 'em onions and et 'em whilst they were worth the bother. Long before the first frosts, they got tougher and tasted more like plain old grass.

Lighting a smoke and remounting, Longarm rode on, and on, until they got to a wide spot in the trail called Parshal. Seeing they had rooms to let over a general store across from the one saloon, Longarm decided to sleep civilized as he pondered his next move.

According to a government survey based in part on the word of once-friendly Indians, mountain men and army scouts, it might be possible to leave the river and ride over the rimrocks to the headwaters of that Yampa, over some bodacious mesas called the Flat Tops and thence on down into the White River Valley. But Longarm had been sent to catch cow thieves stealing government beef, not to run a survey for the government, and he doubted those white trash Tarringtons had ambition to last more than seventy-two hours in the saddle, anyways.

Having seen to the care of his army bays for the night, Longarm found a colored lady vending sweet corn and hush puppies off a pushcart, and when she allowed she had bottled beer as well, he decided it would be smarter to pass on a visit to the nearby saloon. Neither he nor his fresh ponies had been leaving any distinguishing signs along the way. But small town folk remembered strangers in their saloon long after they'd passed on.

Then he heard piano music coming from the saloon. Bad piano music. *Really* bad piano music. So he just had to mosey on over for a closer exanubation.

Standing outside, staring in through the batwing doors, Longarm saw he'd been right about the sources of those awful sounds. A right shapely henna-bottle redhead in a low-cut red velveteen ball gown was seated at the upright piano against the back wall, treating it just awful.

They called the pretty little thing Miss Red Robin as she roamed the West, getting hired to play piano because she was so pretty, and fired because she played piano so awful and wouldn't fuck anybody she didn't like.

Red Robin and Longarm had liked one another, a heap, since she'd tried to kill him down Texas way in the mistaken belief her shooting a fresh boss in Chicago constituted a federal offense.

Since that time things had been friendlier, and on occasion they'd shacked up for nigh a week before they commenced to get on one another's nerves. Red Robin wanted more drama in her life than Longarm was willing to put up with after a gal got to repeating herself.

But he hadn't met up with Red Robin, or any other gals, since he'd enjoyed that pleasantly plump waitress back in Lyons. So he went on in, bellied up to the bar and ordered Maryland rye with a draft chaser if they had it.

They had it, and despite having her bare back to him, Red Robin knew his voice. She hadn't been getting any lately, either.

But being she considered herself a professional, Red Robin gamely finished her rendition of Aura Lee, Lorena or whatever the hell she'd been shooting for, before she rose from her stool to join him at the bar as casually as if they'd come in together, saying, "Evening, you brute. What on earth are you doing here in Parshal of all places?"

Longarm tersely replied, "Just passing through. I was fixing to ask you the same question, Miss Red Robin."

She said, "Call me Robin, seeing you've come in my mouth more than once. I have a real job lined up downstream at Grand Junction. I thought I'd hitched a ride with a sweet old homesteading couple on their way to all that new irrigated land. I got out here after two nights of fighting for my honor in my bedroll. Dirty old *men* are bad enough but have you ever been kissed, French, by a woman with no teeth?"

As a matter of fact, he had and it hadn't been as bad as a man might think, because she'd been pretty, too. But he didn't say this. He said, "I ain't headed far as Grand Junction. But I can carry you far as Rifle, where I got to turn north. You'll only be forty-eight hours from Grand Junction by then."

Red Robin read maps better than she read sheet music. She mused, "That would give us three nights on the trail or, hmmm . . . just the way I like it! When are we leaving, Custis?"

He said, "Daybreak. Got my ponies resting up from a long day on the trail. We'd best pick up another mount for you to ride. Why don't I do that whilst you finish up here and give notice?"

She said they had a deal, and it might have worked out that way if the fat barkeep hadn't moved down their way to tell Red Robin, "I hired you to play that piano or work the johns for drinks, honey. So how come you haven't managed to get this cowboy to buy you a damned beer?"

Red Robin calmly replied, "Fuck you. I don't work here no more and this better man than you doesn't have to buy this girl a drink to get what you've been begging for since you hired me on a Chinaman's wages."

The owner cum barkeep gasped, "You can't quit on me so early, dad blast it! Some boys off the Lazy Zees are riding in special tonight just to hear you!"

Longarm knew the boys had heard how she looked, not how she played. He mildly asked, "How do you brand Lazy Z? Wouldn't a Z on its side look like an N?"

The fat man blared, "How should I know? Do I look like a cowboy, Cowboy? Tell her she can't quit on me like this! Them riders off the Lazy Zees are going to be sore as hell if they ride all this way for nothing!"

Red Robin took Longarm's elbow and said, "Let's go buy me that mule, lover man!"

So once they had, Longarm decided it might be best to wake his army bays and ride on down the river before he wound up with even more pests gunning for him.

They only rode a couple of hours before Longarm tried leading them blind across what smelled and felt underhoof like a sage flat. That was what it turned out to be, and when they came to another one of those granite saucers with a grassy center on the far side, Longarm decided they'd be safe for the night there.

Red Robin wasn't as used to sleeping on the ground, but she proved a mighty good sport about it and had herself buck naked in her high buttoned shoes, with her hair still pinned, by the time Longarm had unrolled the only bedding they had to work with.

So he found her atop the tarp, spread wide in welcome,

by the time he'd shucked his own duds, taking time to settle his shooting irons handy to the overturned saddle they were using as a headboard.

Unless it was raining, you spread a saddle upside down to dry out overnight. The damndest bugs could crawl out of moist soil into warm sweaty leather. He'd spread the unfolded saddle blankets out on bare granite. The two ponies and Red Robin's mule got to browse on the silvery sagebrush they were tethered to. Sheep liked sagebush better than cows or horses did, but it wasn't poisonous as larkspur or locoweed, so what the hell.

It sure beat all how surprising it felt to French kiss a gal with firm pretty teeth after recalling that unusual schoolmarm all the time he'd been getting ready for bed. As he reentered Red Robin, he found he'd lost track of what her old ring dang doo felt like after having entered those others since last they'd gone crazy, atop a hotel bedspread instead of a canvas tarp. When Red Robin said she wanted to get on top, Longarm figured she found the stiff canvas rough on her soft, smooth back and bottom. But when he suggested they get on under the tarp, betwixt his smoother flannel bedding, Red Robin said she liked rough fucking and explained she was out to satisfy a fancy.

So Longarm dismounted, rolled over on his bare back, and allowed the Junoesque henna-bottle redhead to have her wicked way with him.

You had to take Red Robin's word on her natural hair color because she shaved betwixt her legs. When she'd once explained she'd caught crabs in her crotch hair and never wanted to go through that again, Longarm had told her he'd never *asked* how she'd wound up so naked when she took her clothes off.

The "Fancy" she claimed she was indulging just felt like "Gal on Top" from his point of view. It naturally felt swell as Red Robin went to bobbing up and down his love-slicked shaft like a dirty little merry-go-round pony on a shockingly placed brass pole. But as she was going up and down she confided how sometimes, playing piano with hot and sweaty men crowding in all around her, she got to noticing how her clit was swollen without her permit nor desire for any present company, and how wicked it felt to rub her clit back and forth over the edge of a piano stool until she just knew she was fixing to come, smiling up innocently at the men all around. Only it was tougher to come that way than one might think, and sometimes it was all she could do to keep from reaching down to tickle her twat instead of the keyboard.

As if to prove her point Red Robin put one hand down yonder as she balanced on the other, moaning, "Don't look at what I'm doing to my own pussy, Custis! It feels so good but it feels so silly! I doubt I could ever be so depraved with any other man I've ever fucked and I feel so embarrassed doing this with *you*!"

Thrusting up into her, Longarm said soothingly, "Aw, what's a little depravity betwixt friends when they're fucking in private?"

So she whinnied like a mustang mare and jacked off all the way with his old organ grinder up inside her.

Twice.

But later, as they shared a cheroot while the sage-scented night air cooled their fevered flesh, Red Robin sheepishly asked if he thought she was some sort of perverted sex maniac.

To which he could only reply, "I sure do. That's one of the things I've always admired about you, honey."

Chapter 8

Traveling slower, the Tracy Twins had a better than two-day lead on Longarm when they reined in at Glenwood Springs to plan his death there. Assassination got easier when the killers were free to move about unobserved by their target or any possible allies. Pat and Mike took their time, getting the lay of the small settlement as they sent wires, shopped for getaway supplies and gossipped with the locals at the general store cum post office and saloon. Being agreeable gents when they weren't fixing to kill you, they soon found an abandoned cabin on the outskirts of town they could hire by the day for small change from the settlers who'd moved out of it into a better place closer in. They ran the two army bays they'd ridden down from Hot Sulphur Springs into the pole corral out back, spread their bedrolls on the swept dirt floor and kept a small fire going on the freestone hearth to take the damp chill out of the empty shell.

Once they'd settled in, they put up with the tedium that just went with their chosen profession by spelling one another at the shuttered window overlooking the riverside trail down from upstream. It was a pain in the ass they were used to. It helped to study on how much the two of them were fixing to share once they killed the famous Longarm.

Some hard-riding *east* of Longarm and Red Robin, whilst they enjoyed riding together, in and out of the saddle, Buck Tarrington was staring hard-eyed at two cow ponies in a Hot Sulphur Springs corral. Hernando Lopez had made mention of a paint mare and a buckskin gelding and there the two of them were, staring back at him innocent over the top rail of that corral.

Riding around to the front office with his two brothers and four remaining sons in tow, the burly Buck Tarrington dismounted and got right to the point with the old-timer who came out to greet them with a questioning grin.

Buck Tarrington said, "I'll bet you ten dollars you can't tell me where you got that paint mare and the buckskin gelding, Pop."

The older man replied, "You lose. Give me the ten dollars first. Are you the law?"

Tarrington handed over a gold eagle, saying, "Close enough. We're after a tall drink of water with dark hair and mustache. Wears his six-gun cross-draw. Killed a man in Lyons the other day."

The older man whistled as he made the gold piece vanish, saying, "Just goes to show you about books and covers. Struck *me* as a nice young cuss. He traded in those cow ponies for a pair of bigger army bays. You know how the remount service buys mounts as look like they were made with the same cookie cutter from the same gingerbread mix, don't you?"

Buck Tarrington said, "I do. Used to ride one for the Third Colorado. How much of a lead might he have on us, Pop?"

The old-timer thought and decided, "It was Tuesday I sent him on his way aboard one army bay in an army saddle, leading the other bareback. You'll never catch him this side of Grand Junction now."

Buck Tarrington growled, "He ain't going far as Grand Junction and neither are we."

He twisted in his saddle to yell, "You heard this man. Our man went *thataway,* so let's get cracking!"

One of his sons whined, "It's going on noon and our ponies are as hungry and wore out as we are, Dad! When are we ever going to get to eat again?"

Buck Tarrington started to cuss. Then he turned back to the old horse trader and said, "We need seven fresh horses. You can have the seven you see and forty dollars a head for seven more and if you fuck with me about that I'll kill you!"

The old-timer allowed in that case they had a deal. So within half an hour they'd ridden out the far side of Hot Sulphur Springs on bright-eyed and bushy tailed cavalry mounts, eating sandwiches from the general store across from the livery as they rode.

So way downstream, closer to the Tracy Twins than the Tarringtons, Longarm and Red Robin had just enjoyed a set-down noon dinner with a friendly nester and ridden on, hoping to make Glenwood Springs before dark because it was cloudy in the west and al fresco fornication could get tedious in a thunderstorm.

They were way the hell out front of the Tarringtons, albeit she'd never met them and Longarm had about forgotten them by then. They rode most of the afternoon, breaking trail once an hour but resisting the temptation to duck into the trailside trees for a quickie, what with a whole night in town with a roof over their heads just ahead. Being a woman and hence having less self-control, Red Robin did observe that the rubbing back and forth in the saddle was commencing to warm her nature by four in the afternoon. Longarm suggested she try sitting sidesaddle, observing, "That's how come sidesaddles were invented for you ladies to ride more refined. When *menfolk* ride astride, it just makes their balls hurt after a time. I offered to fix you up with a sidesaddle for that mule back there, remember?"

Red Robin smiled like Miss Mona Lisa and said, "A

lot you know about the way young girls fall in love with their ponies! I wish I had a dollar for every twelve year old who came her first time in the saddle. But why are we just *talking* about coming when I see all those cottonwoods just ahead, lover man?"

Longarm glanced casually at the more open scenery down at this drier altitude and said, "It's broad-ass day on close to open range and it's fixing to rain besides. Make more sense if we were to put our slickers on and trot more often instead of talking dirty. You do have a slicker in them carpetbags, I hope?"

She asked in a disgusted tone if he thought she'd just hopped off a boat from the old country. So they rode on some more, and the next time they broke trail he helped her don her yellow oilcloth slicker and broke out his own. They rode on with their rain gear open because the waterproof oilcloth could sweat a rider half to death when it wasn't raining fire and salt. But a little after five Red Robin was glad they hadn't stopped for any quickies as it commenced to *rain fire and salt*.

So the two of them were bundled in yellow oilcloth and they were still getting wet as they loped the last mile downslope into Glenwood Springs.

As they approached the hunting blind of the Tracy Twins, Mike was on watch through the shutters. He called the taller Pat over with a hiss and asked, "What do you think? He's long and he's tall, which is more than any other riders coming by for days can say!"

Pat said, "Madame Fatima wired us to watch for a lonesome rider, headed our way on a cow pony he meant to hire in Lyons. But that tall drink of water's with a woman, two army bays much like our own out back and a fucking mule!"

Mike said, "What if we shot whoever that might be just in case?"

Pat snorted, "What if I shot you to save the boss the

expense of a wire telling me to shoot you? Weren't you paying any mind when I told you we had to *light out* before anyone from town responds to the dulcet tones of our .45–70s? Shoot the wrong Longarm and the real Longarm gets a free pass on down the trail, Mike!"

Mike replied, "Yeah, but what if that's really him? It *could* be him, you know. What if he swapped that cow pony from Lyons for them army bays in Hot Sulphur Springs, the way *we* did?"

"He lives and we live, to kill him another day!" snorted Pat, who added, "Like I said, we get one lick at one rider we can be sure we want to fire on. So hold your fucking fire for now."

Mike muttered morosely, "Got to. The cocksuckers, male and she-male, just got *past* us! Boss is sure going to be cross with us if we've fucked up, Pat!"

His taller sidekick insisted, "Better to be safe than sorry, and like I said, there's always another day. If somebody more convincing don't come along within say twenty-four hours, we can just trail after that mysterious pair. We know where Longarm's *heading,* if that turns out to have been him!"

And so Longarm and Red Robin rode into Glenwood Springs half-soaked but otherwise unmolested, to enjoy a set-down supper and share a steam bath at the hotel, after signing in as Reporter Crawford of the *Denver Post* and wife. When Red Robin asked how come, she agreed Reporter Crawford had it coming as she came with Longarm in the steam bath, standing up.

They were showing off of course. It felt a lot better the old-fashioned way in a feather bed upstairs. Longarm went out of his way to do right by Red Robin and she was as considerate of him, since they knew they'd only have one more night like so together, at the most.

It rained all night. It was raining cold and gray in the morning when the hard-driving Buck Tarrington led his trail-weary clan the last mile into Glenwood Springs, numb with rain chill and in truth disgusted with his own showing off, but what was a hard-riding man of destiny to do when the son of a bitch who owed them blood was somewhere just ahead, dad blast his eyes!

They almost rode past the dark log cabin on the outskirts of town, staring ahead for some place to stop and *eat* for Chrissake. But then Buck Tarrington spotted wood smoke curling from the chimney above the low-pitched roof, swung off the trail for a tighter look at the corral out back and reined in, gasping, "Son of a bitch! There's them two cavalry mounts! He's in that fucking cabin! Spread out, dismount and take cover whilst I do the talking!"

But of course, no professional killer worth his salt is about to let an apparant posse surround his position at its own pace. It was Pat at the window who shouted, "Posse! Can't be nothing but a posse! We've been sold out and I know who sold us! The onliest ones who could know we're in here were the very one's I *wired* about this setup!"

Out on the road, Buck Tarrington was dancing his mount back and forth with the arrogance of a bully who hadn't lost in recent memory as he shouted, "Hello the cabin! We know you're in there, you son of a bitch!"

Then two Springfield .45–70s spoke as one and Buck Tarrington did a backward somersault over his pony's big brown rump to land limp as a dishrag in the mud as his sons and brothers opened fire on the billowing white-black powder smoke–filled windows to either side of the front door.

The squatty Mike yelled, "Shit! I'm hit! Powder River and let her buck!" as he cast his single-shot rifle aside to whip out his six-gun and blaze away, laughing like a mean little kid when he saw one of them rise from the weeds with both hands to his bloody face.

Six furlongs off, Red Robin sat bolt upright in bed, an inspiring sight when a gal built so fine slept stark naked, to gasp, "What was that? It sounded like shooting!"

Longarm propped himself up on one elbow to decide, "It continues to sound like shooting. Somebody is having a gunfight over on the other side of town."

Red Robin asked him what he meant to do about it.

Longarm shrugged his bare shoulders and said, "Not much I *could* do if it was any beeswax of mine. The shots are already commencing to let up. Whatever just happened is already about over and they have a town marshal to worry about local shoot-outs in any case. But seeing you're so wide awake and all excited . . ."

"Stop that, you big goof!" she protested, even as she rolled half atop him to take the matter in hand. So a good time was had by all, at least where *they* were, and by the time he had her begging for more that distant gunfire had faded away.

It was later, sharing flapjacks and sausages downstairs, they got to overhear a garbled version of what had taken place out to the old Flanders place. Longarm warned Red Robin with a look to just sit tight, like himself, when a skinny kid in a black flannel shirt and batwing chaps swaggered in to ask an older man eating at the counter, "You hear about that gunfight out to the Flanders place, Mr. Davis?"

The older man replied, "I sure did. Quirt Rubin told us them two Tracy gents who hired the Flanders place had it out with a bunch of owlhoot riders. You reckon that one Tracy cuss will live?"

The young cowhand said, "Doc Culhane thinks so, if his wound don't mortify. He was only pinked. It was his brother, Mike Tracy, they shot dead more than once. Pat Tracy thinks there were a dozen of 'em. We've tallied seven on the ground and recovered seven ponies. But any left over would have left on horseback, of course."

The man at the counter whistled and replied, "Now ain't that something? But what's Pat Tracy's story? How come him and his brother wound up at feud with all them other strangers?"

The kid said, "He swears he don't know. Says he never laid eyes on any of 'em before. But he's admitted him and his brother were bounty hunters with private detective licenses signed by a Denver judge. He showed his to the marshal. His story is that the two of them came out our way to investigate the stock thefts up to Rio Blanco County."

The older man demurred. "We're way south of Rio Blanco County. Ain't nobody stealing stock down this way!"

The kid said, "Marshal asked him about that. He said they were told somebody down this way might be buying purloined beef run south over the flattops. He says that bunch as killed his brother and scared him half to death might have been trying to stop them from catching somebody doing that."

The older man asked Longarm's question. The kid said Pat Tracy, whoever the blue blazes Pat Tracy might be, was fixing to go back to Denver and discuss the whole case further with the folk who sent him and his late brother out our way in the first place!"

As the kid moved down the counter to order his own breakfast, Red Robin murmured across her flapjacks, "Did any of that make sense to you just now, Custis?"

Longarm shook his head and replied, "Not a lick. I'll wire what just happened to Billy Vail. But I fear that seeing whoever those riders were, they ain't around no more, old Billy will still want me to get it on up to Rio Blanco County."

Red Robin sighed and said, "Pooh, you're no fun. Can we shack up again when we get to Rifle at least?"

He said, "I reckon. Mayhaps nobody will wake us up at the crack of dawn with gunplay next time."

"Next and last time, Custis?" she quietly asked.

He didn't answer. He couldn't come up with anything he knew she'd want to hear.

Chapter 9

Their parting at Rifle was sweet sorrow and timed about perfect. For he'd noticed a certain edge to Red Robin's voice when they supped in Rifle that hadn't been there earlier. He didn't ask what was eating her. He'd long since learned that few if any women knew why they just had to rock the boat after more than a few days of smooth paddling. He suspected it was simply because men and women both deserved something better than one another from Dame Nature.

By noon he was riding and leading alone up the Meeker Trail in the shade of the Grand Hogback, with the morning sun lighting up Monument Peak to his left. He rode all day alone through stark scenery, haunted by the clash of red and white notions of right and wrong. Not far to the west the Ute who'd risen againt Nat Meeker had taken turns raping Nat's wife, daughter and a visiting kinswoman. When the army caught up with them, Chief Colorow had insisted the three white women had been willing. They hadn't put up a fight and nobody had killed them, so what was all the fuss about? That fucking Nat Meeker had plowed up their traditional race course and tried to get them to drink *milk* as if they were infants instead of the bravest fighters of any nation.

Off to the east Longarm knew white and red men had died in greater numbers along the Milk River, twelve cavalry troopers and thirty-seven Ute, in a running gunfight neither side had wanted, for reasons neither understood. Men of goodwill and mean sons of bitches on both sides had simply started shooting with no more understanding of one another than old Don Quixote had displayed against those windmills.

Longarm had long since decided it wasn't anybody's fault that men, women or the different breeds of folk would always misunderstand one another no matter how they tried to get along. White men who said all folk thought the same, or men of any color who thought they really understood women of *any* color were men who hadn't been paying attention to the real world they were stuck with.

As Longarm moved down the far slope into the wide sage flats and tanglewood draws of what had been the North Ute Reserve, he felt torn by the simple justice on both sides of the so-called Indian Question. He could see how the Indians felt about total strangers horning into wide open spaces they'd felt free to roam, enemy raiding parties permitting, and he could see how land-hungry immigrants from many a teeming shore felt about wandering bands of thirty or so hogging space you could set hundreds of prosperous farms on. But the range all about him at the moment was neither-nor. It was still lightly stocked cattle country with a future as uncertain as traditional hunting grounds, and most likely all the farms would be plowed under for mill towns, until the whole world was civilized enough for the big shots who'd clear a forest or flatten a mountain and call it "Progress."

As he forded the White River into the county seat at sundown, he saw they'd progressed the shit out of things since this had all been wide open sagebrush a few short summers back. Meeker wasn't exactly ugly, any more than the asshole it was named for had been exactly evil. The little town, like the man himself, had grown up with limited imagination. Situated on the north bank of the Rio Blanco or White River, Meeker was laid out in a north-south-east-west grid, with a Main Street, a Market Street and streets named after numbers. After riding over forty miles since breakfast, Longarm was too trail-weary to more than see to the care of his ponies at the livery, grab a light set-down supper after checking into the Medicine Horn Hotel on Sixth Street near the post office, wire word of his safe arrival to Billy Vail back in Denver and turn in early with late editions of the *Police Gazette* and a thriller by a Dr. J. H. Robinson of Her Majesty's East Indian Army, called *Hydrabad the Strangler, or Alethe the Child of the Cord*.

He naturally had his McClellan and it's tempting load up in his hired room, draped over the foot of the bed. He hung his six-gun over a bedpost near the head. He made himself a highball with Maryland rye from one of his saddlebags and branch water from the corner washstand. There came an ashtray with the bedside lamp table, but a man who smoked in bed after a forty-mile ride was a man who didn't read the newspapers. So he undressed down to his undershirt, pants and socks so's he could use the facilities down the hall if he had to before he went to sleep, and flopped on the bed to start out with the *Police Gazette*. Line drawings of acrobat gals in tights sure looked shocking when they were printed on pink paper and nobody said for certain they were wearing tights.

The lamplight seemed awfully dim for reading, but the wick didn't need trimming and there was plenty of oil when he hefted it. He saw that the glass chimney had been badly smoked, most likely by an earlier guest not knowing better than to blow an oil lamp out without trimming its wick low first. So he removed the chimney and tore a page he'd already read from the *Police Gazette* to ream all that soot out. After that the lamp shone fine and he got comfortable to read all about Miss Helen Terry, the most beautiful woman in the world, or at least the best-looking actress out of London, currently appearing in a play on State Street in Chicago.

He'd just gotten to what the play was all about, it being one of them drawing room comedies where even the men talked like old biddy hens, when there came some serious knocking on his chamber door. It didn't sound like a raven. Longarm drew his .44–40 from its handy holster as he rolled off the bed to pad across the rug in his socks and stand to one side of the thin paneling and ask who it was.

"Undersheriff Waterford Trumbo of Rio Blanco County!" replied a no-bullshit masculine voice. So Longarm unbolted the door, opened it wide enough to see the star the cuss was wearing on his snuff-colored frock coat and opened wider to let him in.

As Longarm lowerd his gun polite, he saw Trumbo was an older man a tad leaner and shorter than himself. Trumbo's mustache was bigger than Longarm's. So you couldn't see whether he was smiling or not when he said, "We been expecting you for days. When I heard you checked in to the Medicine Horn without calling on us over to the county courthouse, I suspected I'd find you here with a woman or more. But this is important."

Longarm led the way in and put his six-gun away as he replied in a poker playing tone, "I wouldn't want this to get around. But I have been known to turn in alone after a hard day's ride that nigh killed me and two army broncs."

As Longarm carried the fifth of rye and a hotel tumbler over to the washstand, Tumbo nodded knowingly and agreed, "That haul up from Rifle is a pain in the ass either way. No decent campsites if you decide on two twenty-mile slow pokes, and ten miles farther than your average cavalry if you do her in one day. I know how your ass must feel right now. When I heard you'd already wired Denver, I thought I'd best come tell you they're back."

Longarm turned to hand his guest a highball as he asked, "Are we talking about them bad girls? I hadn't heard they were *gone*, ah . . . ?"

Tumbo said, "My friends call me Ford. My mamma never explained how come the grandfather I was named for was named for a town in the old country. I thought you knew the gang them mystery gals seem to be leading raids along the river like a touring vaudeville troup. The same two-week interval betwixt appearances, if you want to call a midnight raid an appearance."

Longarm waved the older lawman to a comfortable seat on the bed and sat astride a handy bentwood chair near the lamp table as Trumbo drew a clearer picture than Henry's onionskins had of the local scene. The local scene as a patchwork quilt of intermountain basins large and small, wet or dry, verdant or bleak depending on local altitude and wind patterns was nigh impossible to picture from as far away as Denver or, hell, one winding mountain range over. Settlers had to know where they were headed and what they were about in the confusion called the Rocky Mountains.

It was said that down around Grand Junction the bottomlands rivaled the rich prairie soils of Iowa and when you stuck an apple seed in wet dirt you had to step back pronto lest you wind up with an apple tree up your pant leg. In other "parks," as local usage described the broader and flatter basins, the dusty soil blew off with the evening breeze if you busted the caliche, or desert crust, with a plow. The wide ranges to either side of the mostly east-to-west White River fell betwixt the two extremes. They were wooded along the river and the creeks that fed into it or atop the ridges where the clouds stubbed their toes, but most of the broad valley soil lay under sagebrush with scattered throw rugs of grassy stretches. The Ute had turned ugly when their agent, Nat Meeker, ordered the dumb but willing Shadrach Price to start plowing a section of short-grass sod the Indians had always used as pony pasture. It hadn't helped when their agent had lectured the complaining Chief Quinkent on the topic of horses, the only things Ute valued more than their womenfolk. Meeker told them they'd just have to get along with fewer ponies. So the Ute had decided to get along with fewer Indian agents, and the rest was tragic history.

The older lawman who lived there now thought the future of Rio Blanco County favored sheep. As a lawman with no dog in that fight, he was more objective about how to make a living off marginal range. He opined, and Longarm had read, they grazed sheep and cows in mixed herds down Australia way. As long as you didn't overstock with *any* grazing critters, grazing could *improve* grasslands, or the fodder as grew among sagebrush, by helping the sunshine get at the growth centers of the grass near the ground. Sheep in sensible numbers didn't go for grass when they could get at the leafy weeds that competed with the same. But when you *did* overstock, sheep naturally et all the weeds and then went after the grass right down to the roots with questing buckteeth that cows lacked.

Sheep started out with that advantage over cows on sagebrush range. More forbs or leafy weeds than grass grew amid the silvery western sage *bushes,* not to be confused with the purple-blooming garden sage of the herb garden. Nobody liked the taste of the yaller-blooming sagebrush much. Sheep browsed it more than cows did. Both browsed it once you overstocked serious. But like the mesquite to the south, sagebrush was an indication you were pushing the range to its limits once there was more sagebrush than anything else.

Trumbo said the N Circle H and other cattle outfits up- or downstream grazed their beef on grass never all that far from a water course whilst more recent stockmen, many of them foreigners, were starting to graze wooly-backs in more modest numbers, so far, on the open sage flats between.

When Longarm asked if the local sheep and cattlemen were at feud, the local lawman shook his head to reply, "Not so far, knock wood. I heard about that range war down Arizona way. But we still have room enough in these parts for folk to raise *ostriches* if they're crazy enough. Have you heard about that asshole out California way who's raising ostriches for their plumes and, according to him, for their *meat*? I ask you, Longarm, would you eat a fucking ostrich?"

Longarm smiled at the picture and said nobody had offered, recent. Then he asked, "You say the mysterious cattle thieves have hit again after how long a lull in their transgressions?"

Trumbo said, "Two weeks. It's almost always two weeks on the nose. They hit Newt Harper's herd during a heavy rain the other night. They ran 'em some damn ways across thick sod, and by morning the rain had washed away any hoofprints or fresh critter turds. We've wired in all directions, with the usual piss poor luck. Them two bad girls seem to vanish cows like stage magicians!"

"Are you dead certain we're talking about *two* bad girls. Not three, or one who changes outfits a lot?"

Trumbo shook his head, took another sip and said, "We've been over that ground ahead of you. There's two of them. They were seen riding side by side, laughing as if they was racing their ponies, with their hair blowing out behind them, by this old Greek sheep man over in Coyote Basin to our northwest."

He took another sip and added, "Mind, this was over a

month ago, before their thieving had everyone up in arms and scouting all over for sign. Since then they ain't been seen as often nor riding so free and easy. But we know it's them, or some men they're leading, because not long after anybody spies one or the other sitting her pony on a distant rise, somebody else loses a dozen head or more!"

"Always cows? Never sheep?" asked Longarm.

Trumbo said, "Always cows. Nobody's missing any pigs or chickens yet. Didn't they tell you we were after bad girls making off with beef, a heap of it already ordered by the government to feed soldiers blue at Fort Duchesne and the new Indian agencies sprouting up along the Green River west of the Utah line?"

Longarm reached out with the bottle to freshen the older man's hotel tumbler as he said, "Been there. Arrested a crooked Indian agent over yonder a spell back. We're talking about where the Great White Father has the *North Ute* parked right now, right?"

Ford Trumbo raised his glass with a nod of thanks to reply, "Well sure, they had to put the fuckers *somewheres,* didn't they? So here's to the horse-raising gang-banging red bastards and let's hope they never come back this way to bother nobody."

Longarm freshened his own drink—it tasted better as you mixed it stronger—and asked, "How do you know they haven't? Assuming there's two bad girls who seem to let themselves be seen now and again, we don't know how many followers they have or what they look like, and if I had to, I reckon I could drive me a cow herd southwest to the new Ute reserves in a week without hurting 'em all that much. Take me half that time to ride back without 'em. But I reckon anybody who'd drop off all that prime beef might be invited to the feast and spend a few days sobering up, don't you?"

Waterford Trumbo stared owl eyed at Longarm as he exploded, "By the great horned spoon, old son, you are just plain *good*! You just got here and you've already got me kicking my own ass for never in this world considering such an obvious possible!"

Longarm shrugged and modestly replied, "Don't feel bad. I'm just as likely full of shit. My boss calls what I'm doing the process of eliminating. You think of all the things that *might* work, then you figure out why they *won't* work, and once you get down to things that *do* work, you're now and again commencing to get warm."

Chapter 10

The book by old Doc Robinson was about that *East* Indian Thuggi tribe as strangled folk in honor of their Goddess Kali, who didn't care if they kept the money, according to the Thuggi priesthood.

Longarm couldn't work up much interest in such goings on outside his jurisdiction, now that he'd talked to Undersheriff Trumbo.

He flopped down with the reading material convinced he would never walk again. Forty miles in the saddle could feel like that to a man's ass and thighs. But after more than a hour's rest, after fodder and water, it was sinking in that his *brain* hardly ever went to bed alone, whilst the world outside was still wide awake and, better yet, half she-male.

So he tossed the book aside and sat up to grump on his boots before he rose to put his shirt, jacket and derringer back on, and strapped on his .44–40 to hunt cow thieves or whatever, grabbing his Stetson on the way out the door.

He went back to the Western Union first, to wire his home office, the War Department and the Bureau of Indian Affairs about his grand notion about purloined beef along the traditional mountain trails of the far-ranging

Ute. The word "Ute" meant something like "Highlander" in Navajo NaDéné. As in the case of the "Apache" or the "Sioux," the BIA had allowed the enemies of the "Ute" to describe them for the records. They tended to call their fool selves *Ho Hada.*

Having done what he could to set up that possible for others, most likely, to eliminate, Longarm sashayed down Main Street toward the sound of music and the municipal corral. The music wasn't coming from the ponies pent up near the river crossing. Somebody was playing the piano, in tune alas, in the Last Chance Saloon across the way.

Longarm circled some to get the lay of the land before entering a strange saloon. Then he went on in to find it crowded for a workday night and bellied his way to the bar through the tobacco smoke and odd musical choices for a Colorado crowd.

Colorado Territory had sided with the Union, serious, and gotten to be a state not long after the otherwise useless Governor Gilpin had forced Harrison's Bummers to lower that Confederate banner flying atop the roof of Wallington & Murphy's store and the First Colorado Cavalry kicked the shit out of Sibley's Texas Brigade at Glorieta Pass. Hence it seemed odd the professor at the upright across from the bar was so good at playing Stephen Foster shit.

Stephen Foster had written heaps of pretty music before the war, but with little imagination when it came to the "Peculiar Institution." To hear Stephen Foster's songs about "Faithful Darkies" one might wonder why the Union Army had bothered.

As Longarm ordered a boilermaker from the blandly pretty barmaid, the professor was playing "Massah's in de Cold Cold Ground." To Longarm's mild surprise, more than one of the regulars wearing his hat crushed Colorado commenced to sing along.

Stephen Foster had been a Northerner. So he hadn't

known slaves as well as the "Massah" in his silly song would have. That was likely why all de darkies was aweeping to think of their slave-driving Massah in de cold cold graveyard ground when he could have had them chopping cotton.

Then Longarm caught on, as the professor and happily loud Colorado riders sang the chorous a second time. It didn't take much to amuse some old boys. But it was worth a dry chuckle to hear them sing . . .

"Down in de cornfield,
Hear dat mournful sound,
All de darkies am a weeping,
My ass is in de cold cold ground!"

Then Longarm's wandering gaze made eye contact with a skinny singer closer to the piano, and as the long drink of water headed back toward the pisser, Longarm left his change by his barely tasted boilermaker's chaser and headed for the front door.

So moments later, as Slender Sam Schneider came out of the slot between the Last Chance and the next-door feed store, intent on a beeline for the corral across the way and a sudden departure from town, he found his path blocked by the just as tall and more seriously built Longarm, who remarked in a kindly tone, "Evening, Slender Sam. I heard you'd got out of Canyon City on good behavior."

The twice convicted cattle thief paused in flight to reply, "I know what you're thinking. It ain't true. I wouldn't know either one of them mystery gals if I woke up in bed with 'em!"

When Longarm didn't answer, Slender Sam insisted, "I'm more anxious than you all to see them cow thieves caught! They've made my life a sad torment since I got out of state prison and rid all the way out here to go straight and start fresh! But thanks to them and that dad blamed *Rocky Mountain News* none of the beef outfits will hire me and I just got fired from the only job I could get, tending dairy cows like a fucking milkmaid!"

"Those bad girls raided a dairy herd?" marveled Longarm.

Slender Sam explained, "You got to knock dairy cows up now and again to get milk outten them. So the widow woman I was working for had some veal calves she was bringing up to sell as beef. She never said nothing but she sure looked at me funny after the first one in her pasture turned up missing. After a second one seemed lost, strayed or stolen close to payday, she paid me as if nothing had happened but said she didn't need me milking her cows and pitching hay no more."

When Longarm still didn't answer, Slender Sam whined, "I ask you the same as I ask her, where in blue lightning could I drive a stolen veal calf overnight and still turn up for breakfast? She agreed it hardly seemed possible I was the one, but she still said she didn't really need that much help around the spread, now that her oldest boy had gotten better at milking. When I asked who she meant to have mowing and pitching hay for her fucking cows, she said she'd been meaning to eat less and get more exercise."

Longarm soberly decided, "It hurts to say this, Slender Sam, but you might have some justice on your side. I'd be proud to have a word in your behalf with this widow woman if it ain't out of my way. Who might she be and where do I find her?"

Slender Sam sighed, "The Widow Ellison, Zelda, I think she said her first name was. Holds a quarter section less than a mile downstream and peddles the produce of her threescore Part-Jersies here in the county seat. Sells eggs, and honey, too. But to save you the bother, I'm off to the Sweetwater Range to the north, come morning. I ain't got no record in Wyoming and I hear they're hiring up by Bitter Creek."

Longarm said he'd heard the same and caught himself before suggesting Slender Sam apply for a job with another widow woman he knew up that way. For he only had Slender Sam's word about going straight and Kim Stover had never done anything to deserve his commending a known thief to her hire. It hadn't been her fault, his fault or anybody's fault that old Kim was one of those women who just didn't feel right fucking gents who didn't want to get married up.

Letting Slender Sam pass with his blessings, Longarm went back into the Last Chance to find not only his schooner of suds but the change he'd left on the bar no longer there.

When he arched a brow and favored the bland barmaid with a frosty smile, she said, "I never. I told Bull Marlow I expected you back on account nobody never leaves me more than a quarter tip. He told me to mind my own beeswax as he helped himself to your beer and that eighty cents. I warned him I'd tell on him if you came back to accuse me of robbing you. But he just laughed and told me he had his Indian blood up and hadn't thought much of you."

Longarm shrugged and said, "I reckon I'll just buy me another beer in that case."

She said, "That's him in the red and black checked shirt and gray hat, over by the piano, grinning at us like a coyote circling sheep."

Longarm shot a quick glance, nodded when he met the bully's knowing eyes, and told the barely passible young thing with mouse-colored hair, "He must have been thirsty. Let's forget it for now. I got more important things on my mind than pushy barflies, ma'am."

She said, "The boys all call me Buttercup, although I

cannot tell you why and . . . What's so funny, mister?"

He said, "My friends call me Custis and that's the very line Miss Buttercup sings in that Gilbert and Sullivan operetta about Queen Victoria's Navy."

"Is she pretty?" asked the Miss Buttercup of Rio Blanco County.

Longarm decided it was safest to say, "Not as pretty as you." And that was the pure truth when you studied on it, for Poor Little Buttercup in *H.M.S. Pinafore* was an ugly old hag working behind a pushcart on the docks instead of a bar in the Last Chance.

His gallant fib seemed to cheer this other Miss Buttercup a heap. She'd already confessed she wasn't used to getting big tips.

The professor was playing the one about "Old Black Joe" now. It beat all how sentimental Southerners could still listen to that one without laughing. The Colorado crowd was naturally more amused by the notion of a humble old darkie missing his dead masters and looking forward to joining them in Heaven after a lifetime of slavery on Earth, with a view to serving them some more as in times gone by. The chorus was supposed to go . . .

"I's comin'!
I's comin'!
Though my head am bending low,
I hears their gentle voices callin' . . .
Old . . . Black . . . Joe."

It sounded even sillier when everybody loudly sang . . .

"I hears their gentle voices callin' . . .
Get your black ass up here, you fool nigger!"

Miss Buttercup slid a tumbler of rye across the bar beside his barely sipped beer and moved to put a new head on the beer as she murmured before he could say anything, "On the house. Then you'd better leave. I've seen that look in Bull Marlow's eye before . . . Custis. Bull can be awfully mean when he thinks he has the Indian sign on somebody, and you shouldn't have nodded friendly at him like that. I 'spect he thinks you're scared of him, now!"

Longarm asked, "You ever hear of a Widow Ellison as sells dairy produce and eggs around here, Miss Buttercup?"

She said, "Sure. We buy the cream for our coffee off old Zelda. She's all right. Her man got gored to death by a Jersey bull shortly after they got here. The Ellisons were one of the first white families here in Meeker. I know how come you asked. But it ain't true about her milking hands and those lying riders off the Rocking T."

"Is she that good-looking?" Longarm asked, wearily adding, "You're always hearing dirty stories about women alone, unless they're sort of plain, and I've heard shockers about downright homely schoolmarms."

Miss Buttercup sighed and said, "Wait till you hear about me and a whole cavalry troop I served here this spring, the way I'm serving you right now, I mean."

She looked away and sighed. "Nary a one of 'em even asked my name." Then she stared owl-eyed past Longarm to gasp, "Oh, Lord, he's on his way and you'd better run, Custis!"

Longarm just turned his back to her to lean it against the bar and face Bull Marlow as the bully of the town came their way with an empty schooner in his hand. The piano music behind him died with a whimper as Bull Marlow held the empty out to Longarm, saying, "I seem to have drunk all your beer here, pard. Would you care to buy me another?"

Longarm calmly replied, "Not hardly. Why don't you use some of the small change you stole from me like the sneak thief you were born?"

Bull Marlow swung the glass beer schooner at Longarm's head, just as everyone in the Last Chance, including Longarm, had expected.

It was the usual roundhouse right of the strong but unskilled saloon brawler, distinguished only by its lethal load of breakable glass. Longarm blocked with the beer schooner in his own left fist. Foaming beer flew every which way as the heavy base of Longarm's big schooner met Bull Marlow's incoming forearm a quarter of the way up from the wrist, where the radius bone was thinnest, snapping it like a twig with an audible pop as Longarm threw his own right cross.

Bull Marlow was screaming in pain from his busted arm when Longarm fed him an open mouth full of knuckles. It hurt Longarm's fist a heap, but he wasn't the one losing all those teeth, so what the hell.

Longarm hadn't busted his beer schooner, so he put it back on the bar and said, "I could use a refill, Miss Buttercup," as Bull Marlow rolled around in the sawdust at his feet like an earthworm caught by the morning sun on a flagstone walk, yelling he'd been assassinated as far as they could make out. It was hard to hear exact words when a man was spitting blood and teeth through lips that swollen.

Nobody else had a thing to say until someone in the back said a mean thing about busting a man in the mouth after you'd already busted his poor arm. But an older and wiser voice warned, "Stay out of it, cowboy! Don't you know who Bull just fucked with?"

Another regular said, "Ford Trumbo *said* they were sending in that famous federal gun and he's heeled with a double-action .44–40! So all in all Bull's lucky to be alive and this here fight is all Bull's own to keep and cherish!"

By the time Miss Buttercup had refilled Longarm's beer schooner they could all see Bull Marlow was in poor shape. The bleeding was getting no better and his blubbering sounded weaker. Longarm sighed and asked, "Is there a doctor in the house? I'll pay within reason for such damages as I may have done to him my ownself. But if he's suffering consumption or a social disease he's on his own."

A crusty old gnome in a rusty black suit came out of the crowd with his black bag to declare, "I'm a fair veterinarian and I reckon if I can save a four-legged jackass I can keep this two-legged jackass from dying. But are you sure you *want* me to, stranger? I know this mean cuss better than you, and if you figure he's going to be at all *grateful* to such a good sport, you got another think coming!"

Another voice in the crowd chimed in, "That's for sure. Bull Marlow has been known to bust a chair over the head of a total innocent who never said a word to him! How do you expect him to feel about a man who just busted his arm and knocked out half his teeth?"

Chapter 11

Longarm had played enough poker to quit whilst he was ahead, and thanks to two boilermakers, the dullness of Doc Robinson's thriller about murdersome Thuggi, and the aftereffects of that forty-mile ride coming back as the excitement wore off, Longarm lay slugbed until six A.M. and would have slept longer if Undersheriff Trumbo hadn't come back with the town law, a Marshal Price who said it was all right to call him Dad, like everyone else did.

Dad Price was naturally curious as to the details of Bull Marlow's hard night. Longarm was, too. So betwixt them they established that that horse doctor had set the bully's arm in a plaster cast, pulled the looser stubs of his busted teeth and prescribed bed rest with rye whiskey and the fat old breed gal who loved him despite all his faults.

Bull Marlow didn't have a regular job. That was why he extorted drinks from smaller men or stole change right off the bar. It happened often, according to Dad Price. But nobody up until the night before had stood up to Bull Marlow, since the night he'd hospitalized all six foot six of Leroy Vogel, the ramrod of the Lazy Eight.

Dad Price opined, and Undersheriff Trumbo agreed, that Longarm should have killed the burly bastard when he'd had the justification. Price said, "He was assaulting you unprovoked with a deadly weapon and you had on that .44–40! Wild Bill or Bat Masterson would have shot him down like a dog!"

Longarm shrugged and said, "I ain't out to shoot pesky drunks. Gets to be a bad habit, like bragging on how many whores you've seducted."

Dad Price said, "The boys at the Last Chance all agree you were a real sport after Bull stole your beer and your money and tried to brain you. But if you're expecting *Bull* to be a good sport about it, once he's on his feet again, forget it! He's poison mean to folk who've never done nothing to him, and a spite holder of the first water. The minute he feels up to it, Bull's going to try and pay you back, and it's an established fact he fights dirty!"

Longarm shrugged as he finished buttoning his shirt and said, "With any luck I'll be finished up this way by the time he feels up to it. I'll be out on the range a heap of my time in these parts, eliminating. Now that I've got here, I see the typewritten reports I read along the way failed to picture the lay of the land in detail. Before I ride out of town to pester other folk, I'd like to go over your own complaints and see if I can X 'em on my government survey map."

Undersheriff Trumbo said, "No need to go to all that trouble. I can let you have a map of Rio Blanco County already Xed, except we drew circles around each home spread that's been hit."

As Longarm strapped on his six-gun, Trumbo added, "We ordered a score of maps from the printing office and there wasn't that many circles to draw. Newt Harper's N Circle H has been hit hard and often. Nobody else has lost more than a few head hither and yon, all downstream west of town and mostly north of the river."

"Mostly? Not all?" asked Longarm.

Trumbo said, "The Lazy Four to the south of Harper's

N Circle H has lost mayhaps half a dozen head. They said they wasn't certain because they have some tanglewood draws. I told 'em to come back when they had a tighter tally to offer us. Can't hardly posse up to chase strays in tanglewood, for all one knows, when you can't even say how many you may be after!"

"What difference does the side of the river make?" asked Dad Price.

Longarm said, "Looking for patterns. This fire chief I know says a fire bug sets fires within a short dash from his own cover or way off in other neighborhoods. Seldom *both.* We figure Frank and Jesse are still dropping by their old haunts in Clay County, Missouri, because they never rob anybody in Clay County."

Dad Price asked, "Are you saying you suspect somebody holed up on the south side of the river might be stealing cows on the north side to confound us?"

Longarm said, "Too early to say. If that Lazy Four's been hit by the same cow thieves and they ain't hit all that many north of the river, there may be no pattern worth mention. I'll just mosey downstream and make some more notes after I walk you gents over to pick up that map. I just hate to make notes. But we all know we got to unless we aim to run in circles like fools until the ones we're after call out to us from their hiding places to help us out."

The two older lawmen chuckled wearily in agreement. Trumbo sighed. "It has to be somebody hiding two-faced in plain sight. For we've yet to find the considerable campsite outsiders would have left for us to find by this time if they were riding in and out from other parts. The mystery ain't how they're doing it in the dead of the night. The mystery is where in blue thunder they're *selling* the fucking beef! Ain't but a handful of butchers in the county, and nobody's been running a sale on prime ribs. So they got to be moving it out of the county, and no matter how you slice that, it's impossible!"

Price nodded and said, "Can't have her two ways. Them mysterious bad girls have to get off them ponies now and again to brew some coffee or at least take a shit. Cows run off in any numbers leave hoofprints as well as shit in their wake. So how come nobody's been able to cut a lick of sign in any direction? The riders trying ain't Sunday school teachers. They're mostly *cattlemen,* and the sheepherders offering to help know a thing or two about moving critters with hard hooves over marginal range!"

Longarm was too polite to tell them they were running around in that circle he'd mentioned. He walked them over to the courthouse square and accepted a stirrup cup from a file drawer marked B for Bourbon before he returned to the Medicine Horn for his riding gear, with the survey map he'd needed more than a drink.

He carried it all over to the livery and saddled one of his army bays. He felt no call to ride out with two ponies, after a casual examination of the penciled-in sites on the printed map.

When you rode down the wagon trace to Rangely, no more than two bare dusty ruts a standard axle width apart, it made more sense in person than across map paper. Rangely lay forty-five miles to the west by crow. It was miles farther when you followed the river way to the north before it passed Rangely at nigh the same latitude as the county seat, and after that, Rangely lay *south* of the river. So anyone staring down at the fool map could see fording the river south of Meeker to beeline due west across that big bend would save you a whole lot of miles.

But not a whole lot of *trouble,* when you gazed about you from the saddle, following the advice of the wagon trace.

For the lay of the land to the north horizon was semiarid rolling rises the rain clouds from the west-north-west barely noticed, whilst the higher country Longarm had ridden north across the day before rose serious enough to water many a draw, three of them serious if not dangerous when in flood, along that easy pencil line across paper. It made way more sense to move a wagon, or even stock, along the drier northern banks of the White River.

It was called a white river, or Rio Blanco, because of the way it foamed white over many a stretch of rapid. Where it ran smoother, the water was clear as crystal. Cottonwood and crack willow grew thick along the water's edge, but on the higher ground the wagon trace was following you saw way more sagebrush than grass within easy riding of Meeker.

So Longarm knew somebody had gone to a whole lot of trouble as they approached a fenced-in quarter section, neatly divided into four forty-acre plots by the same unrusted barbwire. A sunflower windmill nigh the low-slung log construction in the corner closer to town accounted for the green grass fenced in that late in the summer on sagebrush range. From the saddle, riding in, Longarm was guessing they'd drilled in timothy and fescue seed along with some no-shit red clover. He saw that the twoscore dairy cows Slender Sam had mentioned were all pent on one forty, north of the house and barnyard. Someone had even painted the shutters and Dutch door of the main house a cheerful apple green. It hardly seemed fair a just Lord would allow a nester with all that ambition to be gored. But they did say the most famous Spanish bullfighters refused to get in the ring with a dairy bull, and the Jersey breed was said to be most dangerous of all.

As he rode into their dooryard, braced for the usual yapping from the usual yard dogs, nobody yapped at him and he saw a girl of around six in a white muslin pinafore trying to spin a rope near the hitching rail. She smiled up at him uncertainly as he reined in. He howdied her and she said, "Do you know how you spin these infernal ropes, Mister Cowboy? My big brother can spin one like anything but I can't get this one to mind at all!"

As he dismounted to tether his bay, he told her he'd try, knowing what she was doing wrong. Most men, women and children made the same mistake after they'd watched a vaudeville cowboy twirl his trick rope like so. He said, "Secret is in our wrists. Would you let me show you, ma'am?"

The brown-haired tyke handed her fathom of clothesline over, saying, "Aw, I aint no ma'am. My name is Zenobia and I'm going on seven years old, so there, but you can try if you've a mind to."

Longarm took the limp noose and eighteen inches or so of pay-out from Zenobia and commenced to twirl the noose as a fair circle, as he told her, "Don't watch the rope. Watch my wrist. When you hold the rope with your wrist straight and try to twirl her, the pay-out can't turn with the noose so it kinks, like so!"

He locked his wrist to make a tangled hash of his loop. Then he got it to spinning gracefully again, explaining, "See what my wrist is doing, Miss Zenobia? My *hand* stays with the rope it's holding as my *wrist* tags after both in the same circle. Try to make your wrist move like a *swivel* and—"

"May I *help* you, good sir?" came a voice from the open top of the Dutch door at about ten below zero. It added, "The man of the house is in town on an errand but we're expecting him back any moment!"

Longarm gave the trick rope back to its diminutive owner as he ticked his hat brim to the lady of the house and told her who he was.

Zelda Ellison was a shade darker haired than her rope-spinning girl child and built a heap more tempting. He believed she'd told Slender Sam she was out to lose a few pounds by working harder, albeit what she was packing on her five foot six or seven seemed muscular as a woman with natural feelings might manage. Her tits looked solid and about the same size as a pair of grapefruit halves under her own thin white cotton smock. It was neatly hand-sewn and she'd used a heap of bleach, but he could still make out the brand sack the thrifty gal had salvaged once the flour had been done away with.

The tall, unpainted pretty thing with her dark brown hair in pigtails like her daughter's said if he was the law and wanted to talk to her about her missing veal calves he'd best come on in for coffee and cake whilst he was about it.

She opened the lower leaf of her Dutch door to admit him. As he followed her inside, Longarm saw the log walls inside had been whitewashed, and the place had the clean smell of pine oil and naptha soap that went with the constant boiling and scrubbing of a well-run dairy farm. When hardworking nesters knew what they were doing they could sell ten gallons of cream for more than an acre of grain. But when they didn't know what they were doing, they couldn't *give* spoilt milk produce away.

The young widow woman sat him at a never-painted-often-scrubbed pine table, and as she warmed the coffee on the front plate and sliced some pound cake on a bread-board, Longarm brought her up to date on his conversation with Slender Sam Schneider. She confirmed Schneider's suspicions that she'd let him go when she suspected he'd been the one who'd stolen her veal, more than once.

She said, "We were taken in, the more fools us. We both knew better, but we thought it our Christian duty to help a fallen sinner who'd seen the light find his way back. I knew the moment I laid eyes on Samuel that he was a leopard who couldn't change his spots. But against my better judgment I gave him a chance, and when we were missing a veal calf before his first week out here was up, I thought he understood I had my eye on him, but—"

"Who might *we* be, Miss Zelda?" Longarm cut in.

She said, "Helena Gorse over to Meeker." She continued, explaining, "Helena and me 'tend the same First Congregational in town. She runs a boardinghouse over yonder and when that sniveling Samuel Schneider confessed to her he'd just got out of state prison and showed her a letter from the prison chaplain asking any good Congregationalist to give a repentent thief a chance, Helena sent him out here to me, she having no position for a hand who handled stock."

She placed his coffee and cake before Longarm and sat down across the table from him with only a cup as she bitterly continued, "He handled stock indeed, right through the wire he'd cut and resplice in the dead of the night! The fool thought a woman who'd helped her man string every yard of that barbwire wouldn't notice where it had been cut and respliced."

"You read any other sign over yonder, ma'am?" Longarm asked.

She shrugged and asked, "Wasn't that enough? He shifted stock, both times, while it was raining. With nobody grazing range stock close to our property line, my poor little veal calves never busted the wet sod betwixt the sagebrush clumps all around. Samuel could have led them both like *pets* in most any direction after that."

Longarm didn't ask what an ex-convict who bunked on a spread would do with a pet calf on or off the property.

Outside, little Zenobia was yelling fit to bust. Both adults rose to move over to the door. The little gal was twirling her clothesline like a fancy trick roper, grinning like mad as she chortled, "I can do it! I can do it! Look at me *doing* it, Momma!"

Zelda Ellison turned to Longarm to murmur, "Thank you. I'm sorry I behaved so suspisciously toward you, before, Deputy Long."

Longarm said, "My friends call me Custis, and you were right to wonder what a strange man was doing with your girl child, Miss Zelda. Lord knows we got a heap of suspicious characters pussyfooting around out yonder!"

Chapter 12

Longarm was coffee and caked at all the places he stopped, and he had to stop at all the circled brands on the sheriff's department map. So he never worried about dinner as the sun arched over him to commence the afternoon and he kept wending his way west, not a lick wiser than he'd started out.

The bigger N Circle H that had been hit hardest lay an easy ride east of Rangely, near the state line. So Longarm figured he faced a night in his bedroll on open range, but that was how come he'd lashed a bedroll behind the cantle of his McClellan. When it commenced to cloud in the west as he rode into it, he reflected he'd packed his slicker with *that* possible in mind. He rode into the N Circle H late in the afternoon and got invited to sleep dry. Galloping through rain had sleeping in it beat. Longarm had to also accept an invite to supper, even though his gut was sloshing with coffee and cake he'd had by that time. He accepted so as to look old Newt Harper over when the bluff cattle baron wasn't talking like the good old boy he played so natural it had to be an act.

Newton Harper was a big paunchy cuss of around forty-five, with a graying walrus mustache that made it tough to tell if he was really smiling or not. He shook with a grip so firm he had to be putting his back into it, and Longarm was no sooner off his bay and in the big log house before the owner produced more papers than Longarm had asked to see. Newt showed him his Land Office homestead claim as well as that government beef contract. He said, "I know what you and Uncle Sam are thinking, Deputy Long. So I'll show you my bills of sale on the cows I druv down from the Sweetwater range."

As Longarm accepted the sheaf of papers, seated comfortably by the cold fireplace with a bourbon and branch water handy, he asked, "What am I supposed to be thinking, Mr. Harper?"

The bluff stockman said, "Call me Newt. You federal men suspect I never had the beef I agreed to provide to Fort Duchesne in the first place, right?"

Longarm frowned in puzzlement and asked, "How come you're worried about anyone suspecting that? Your government contract offers no tally of the herd you have *on hand*. It says you've agreed to provide beef on the hoof at a steady rate to the Fort Duchesne mess officer. The army contracts the same general terms all over. That mess officer don't care how many cows you might have or whether you have any cows at all. He wants you to provide him with regular beef rations for a squadron of cavalry and their dependents. Where you round it up is up to you."

Newt Harper replied in an injured tone, "I heard of all the fuss down Lincoln County way when Uncle John Chisum accused Larry Murphy of providing Fort Stanton and that Mescarelo Agency with Chisum beef. I'll have you know every critter we've druv over to Fort Duchesne to date was wearing my very own N Circle H and no other brand at all! You can ask 'em at Fort Duchesne if you want!"

Longarm made a mental note to do just that. Nobody

in Rio Blanco was accusing Harper of shit. He was the one whose complaints had set the federal millstones to grinding. Longarm wondered what the older man had on his conscience.

Longarm told himself not to jump into that puddle with both feet. A lot of self-made men, as well as men who were still trying, tended to talk too much and try too hard, making up war records nobody gave toad squat about or winning games they'd never played. Newt Harper was as likely one of those old boys who bragged about fucking the schoolmarm who'd never smiled at 'em or assured a friend he was not out to fuck his wife before anyone thought to ask.

Their Chinee cook had been fixing to serve supper out back in the evening breeze, but with summer rain falling warm as his tea they supped in a big old open-sided mess tent Newt said he'd bought off the army as beyond their repair. Newt allowed and Longarm had to agree it would have been dumb to tear up a tent that only needed some patching.

But the smell of the new beeswax and turpentine waterproofing hardly made a man already full of coffee and cake hunger after sourdough biscuits, salt pork and beans. So he toyed with his grub as he watched the interplay betwixt old Newt and his hands. They acted like good old boys who wanted it understood *they* had nothing to hide.

He decided they *were* simply semiliterate country boys aware of their own shortcomings, when he couldn't for the life of him figure out what they could have to feel defensive about, save for the way they et with their knives.

A golden sunset suddenly replaced the warm shower as the summer storm let up without a thunderclap of comment.

Without waiting for any comment from his guest, Newt Harper told Longarm, "It's too late to ride on, even if it's stopped for good. I told you you'd be bunking in the big house, dammit!"

Longarm smiled uncertainly and decided, "I was brung up by kind but thrifty parents who warned me to waste not and want not, Newt. I got well over an hour's worth of light left to ride by and I thought I might camp over by the Cathedral Bluffs and mayhaps scout for Indian sign before I call it a day."

Newt Harper snorted, "You won't find Indian sign over yonder now! Not *fresh* Indian sign, leastways. Army has 'em all across the Green River by now, if they know what's good for 'em!"

One of his riders snorted, "Met up with some Fifth Cav downstream a ways a month ago. They told us they've cleaned out all the Ute south of the river and ain't been able to find none *north* of the river. So I reckon there's hardly any left to either side, right?"

Longarm quietly pointed out, "*Hardly* any ain't the same as none at all."

From his head of the table Newt Harper demanded, "What do any of us care about ragged-ass Indians, Longarm? Are you saying you suspect Ute Indians are in cahoots with them bad girls who keep stealing my cows?"

Longarm said, "I'm eliminating. The Ute never turned on Nat Meeker because he wanted them to *eat* cows. They just never wanted to *milk* any. In their shining times they valued elk and venison, in that order. A cow makes a passible substitute for an elk, and there ain't nigh as many elk out this way as there used to be."

He sipped some not-bad black coffee and added, "That's a sticking point Mister Lo can't seem to master. Folk can only live by hunting and food gathering in limited numbers over county-sized hunting grounds for bands of say thirty families. The noble savage way of life worked fair enough up to the time Mister Lo got the white man's horses and iron hardware to hunt with. Like it or not, and Mister Lo sure seems to hate the notion, there just ain't enough hunting ground on the North American continent to support the population explosion of the Indians alone, as hunters and gatherers. But whilst they're figuring this out we can look forward to increasing raids by ever larger bands with ever more kids to feed. So, like I said, I'd best eliminate hold-out Ute the army ain't rounded up yet."

Newt Harper asked, "What about them white gals scouting for the cow thieves? Are you suggesting them bad girls are renegade whites as well as just plain bad?"

Longarm said, "Ain't suggesting. Eliminating. How does anybody know for certain they're *white*? Didn't some Mormon Danites pretend to be Indians at the massacre of Mountain Meadows back in '57? It's duck soup simple to dress like anything when you don't let folk see you up close. For all we really know those bad girls could be bad *boys* until I can eliminate *that*!"

He added, "I mean to ford the river and have me a talk with your neighbors at the Lazy Four on my way to the Cathedral Bluffs. What can you tell me about their losses to those cow thieves, Newt?"

Harper shrugged and said, "Not much. We just got here and they keep to themselves. I suspect they might be Mormons, or even Papists. I understand they shop most in Rangely. When they do, they ride downstream on the far side. Save's 'em a ford both ways. I sent them an invite to a housewarming when first we arrived. They sent back word they were too busy. Never said what they were busy *at* over yonder. Maybe they're bees. Their name's Watson, I hear tell. I can't tell you much more than that."

Longarm allowed he'd ask the Watsons about anything Newt Harper had left out. Then he finished his black coffee and excused himself to get on across the river whilst there was still some daylight left.

As he followed the young wrangler over to their corral

to get his army bay, Longarm casually asked how come he hadn't noticed too many women and children on the N Circle H, seeing it was a home spread.

The kid said, "Riders from other outfits are forever asking us about that. We ain't a bunch of fairies. We just got here. Old Newt left a wife up Wyoming way, I hear. I wasn't riding for him when they druv the consolidated herd south to claim all this Indian land. So I just can't say whether she refused to come along as some say or whether he means to send for her when things get more organized, the way others have it."

Longarm had no call to puruse that line of questioning further. It was none of his beeswax to begin with, and whether Newt Harper was a happily married man or a big sissy had no bearing on his losses to those mysterious raiders, red or white.

Thanking the young wrangler and mounting his watered, foddered and rested bay, Longarm rode due south the short way to the river and explored downstream along the wooded banks to where he found a calmer stretch flowing over acres of gravel you could see through the clear mountain snowmelt, barely stirrup deep.

They forged across and up the far bank through a growth of alder and willow, to bust out on the far side where, setting a palomino atop a not too distant rise, Longarm spied what surely looked like a gal in a tan whipcord riding habit, setting sidesaddle as she stared back at him like she and her pony were posing in the soft gloaming light.

She wore no hat. Her long unbound hair hung down over her shoulders the same color as her blond pony. As Longarm howdied her with a wave, she never waved back. She reined her mount casually round to the south to walk it, not run it, out of sight off that rise.

Longarm knew she'd quirt her mount into a dead run as soon as he couldn't see her. So he heeled his bay and whupped its brown rump with the ends of his own reins to charge up that rise like a member of that famous Light Brigade.

Had he had a bugle handy he'd have been blowing it.

As he topped the rise, he saw that sure enough the strange gal on the palomino was halfway up the next one, at full gallop. So he whupped his bay down into the draw between, going downhill way faster on its longer legs. It was a good old vet despite its age, and in spite of romantic notions to the contrary, the army remount service seldom bought horseflesh that wasn't bigger, stronger and faster than your average Indian or cow pony. So he and doubtless the gal topping the far rise on that palomino knew Longarm's army mount had the edge in a long-distance lope across open range.

So she reined in up yonder, as if taunting him or waiting up for him, and as he loped up the next slope toward her she called out, "I'll have you know I'm Miss Fiona Watson of the Lazy Four and if you rape me I'll tell all four of my uncles and you will never in this world get out of these mountains alive, good sir!"

Longarm slowed to a walk, so as to call back in a steadier tone that he wasn't a good sir but only the law. As he joined her atop the grass-grown ridge in the soft evening breeze, her free falling blond hair was blowing in the same and she looked tempting as peaches and cream. He figured her for around seventeen, soaking wet, as he tried not to stare at her cupcakes whilst he offered her his name and told her what he was doing on her side of the river.

She gestured into the sunset with her braided rawhide riding quirt to imperiously proclaim, "You will find our homestead three rises to the west, and there you shall surely find a warm welcome. For we Watsons are not slow. But you shall have to introduce yourself, Deputy Long, for I am eastward bound and as you see there's not much light left."

He nodded but asked where she hoped to get to before full dark, adding, "There's no moonlight promised for tonight, and if you're on your way to Meeker it's a good twenty-five miles or more."

She dimpled and said, "You're right. It's more. But I am on my way to the Hundred and Ten, if you must know, to visit a friend who's been feeling poorly with some female medication I'd as soon not talk about."

Longarm said in that case they'd say no more about it. He ticked his hat brim to the pretty little snip, and she reined her palomino away and gave it a good smack on the rump, to canter off to the east without so much as a kiss my ass.

Longarm smiled thinly and muttered, "Hope you *both* suffer female troubles till you learn some manners," as he swung his own mount's head to the west and rode into the sunset at a walk where they were moving level or uphill and a trot where the slope favored that gait.

As the imperious young gal had promised, they hadn't gone far and it was still light enough to make out colors when they topped another rise to see the welcoming sprawl of the Lazy Four ahead.

Someone down yonder spotted Longarm on the skyline. So as he came in more than one figure came out into the dooryard to greet him. As he got within hailing distance a jovial male voice called out to him, "You just missed supper, stranger. But we might manage some warmed over Mulligan for you and we've always got coffee on the range out back."

As he dismounted near the sprawly main house, Longarm declared he'd had his supper. A wrangler came forward to take charge of his mount. So as Longarm shook with the nearest of the four lazy Watson brothers, he told them who he was, what he was doing there, and added he'd just met up with their niece, Miss Fiona, out on the range.

All four of the slightly older stockmen, who seemed to have been formed from the same batter and with the same clean-cutting cookie mold, exchanged puzzled glances. The one Longarm had just shaken with told him, "Onliest niece around here is inside with the other womenkind, Deputy Long. She'd be nine years old and her name is Edith. Did I say something wrong, Deputy Long? You're staring at me like I just now slapped you across the face with a dead fish!"

To which Longarm could only reply, "You just did. Have you ever had the feeling you've been screwed, blewed and tattooed by a two-faced woman?"

All four of the older men chuckled knowingly. One sighed and said, "Show me the man who's never been played for a sucker by a woman and I will show you a man who likes boys better! But why on earth would any gal want to declare she was kin to us old boys when she wasn't?"

Longarm said, "To make a total sap out of this child, of course. I had the drop on one of those stranger gals that other folk have been seeing at a distance. I was close enough I could have grabbed her if I hadn't been so trusting I let her ride off, laughing at me!"

Chapter 13

Longarm spent the night among the cozy confines of the Lazy Four's extended family of four easygoing rather than really lazy Watson brothers and *their* extended families. The kids all turned in early so the grownups could stay up late and talk in circles about the brazen behavior of that bad girl, if she was one of those bad girls, who'd called herself Fiona Watson on her way to visit the nearby Hundred and Ten brand. None of the Watsons knew any gal named Fiona. The Watsons said they'd been Lowland Scots in the old country and that Fiona was a Highland name. The gal on the palomino hadn't likely known that as she grabbed for a Scotch name out of thin air. One of the brothers got a brand book to check before he declared once and for all there was no Hundred and Ten brand registered anywhere in Colorado. Another one recalled hearing of a famous Hundred and *One* brand out California way. Biggest "rancho" in the state to hear some tell. They found Longarm's up-close description of the pretty little thing interesting, and all agreed she didn't work so well leading or scouting for hold-out Ute stock raiders. Albeit one of the Watson wives sniffed and reminded them all how Simon Girty, a pure Scotch-Irish son of a bitch, had led Shawnee scalping parties against his own kind back in the time of the Revolution.

Next morning, after bacon and eggs, Longarm backtracked in a vain attempt to cut sign. But searching for distinctive hoofprints on sod ranged by herds of cattle and wilder hooves was sort of like trying to determine who'd last pissed in the alley behind a saloon of a payday night.

So Longarm swung around to ride southwest toward the Cathedral Bluffs, crossing more than one headwater creek of the Piceance.

All the folded up geology had started out the same mile-thick layer cake of sedimentary rock over gray granite basement rock. Prospectors looked for veins of lead, zinc, copper, silver or gold in that order where the potato piles of granite punched through all the shit above. Slabs of sandstone, and even more shale, formed tilty hogbacks or flat-topped mesas all around the flanks of the granite massifs. You got beds of limestone, slate, some coal and even rock oil where there'd once been puddles and lagoons of stagnant water for a million years or so, before more time, heat and pressure had turned it all to the rocks of the Rocky Mountains. So the Cathedral Bluffs rose as a fair imitation of Gothic spires and buttresses along the southwest flanks of the Piceance Valley.

Longarm spent more time drifing back and forth across the flat valley floor, seeking sign amid the sage and rabbit brush.

There was plenty of sign reading those parts had once been a lot more occupied by Indians. He rode past many a long burnt-out campfire, the empty holes of pulled up stakes and tepee poles and, wistfully, a corn-husk doll dropped by some Indian girl-child as her kin ran away from soldiers blue. When Indians were just *herded* off to a reserve by the cavalry, they seldom dropped shit.

Longarm rode on, searching for the trail over the Cathedral Bluffs that had to be there. The morning sun shone into the eyes of anybody staring east from any of those hundred of natural lookouts. Longarm was just as glad. The newspapers *said* the agreed-to relocation of the Ute had been going according to plan, with the last of them due to be out of Colorado for good within another year at the most. But Indians didn't all read newspapers, and had all the Ute been all that obedient to begin with, Governor Pitkin never could have pushed that evacuation ordinance through in the first place.

Longarm knew that if there were any quill Indians hiding out around their traditional Colorado hunting grounds they'd be finding it tough to hunt enough wild game to matter, and that would account for a heap of missing beef that didn't seem to be turning up for sale anywheres. He couldn't see how at least one white gal and possibly another fit in with feeding hold-out Indians in some lonesome Colorado valley, and if that was it, they were talking about a whole lot of Indians indeed. One side of beef could feed your average family of anybody for weeks if they had an ice or smokehouse. Newt Harper alone had lost eight hundred head, or more than enough to feed the garrison over at Fort Duchesne and the new Ute agency to the south along the Green River for the rest of the damned year.

Longarm found a beaten path across his route and turned to follow it toward what turned out to be a narrow cleft in the tightly packed columns ahead. Drawing his saddle gun and levering a round in its chamber, Longarm rested it across his spread thighs with his gun hand on the trigger as he took a deep breath and lit into the gloomy slit toward the southwest. But nobody pegged a shot or dropped a boulder from the bluffs to either side, and as he rode the bluffs got lower and lower until he was up under the open sky again, riding across patches of red sandstone outcrop betwixt acres of sagebrush or, hither and yon, a grove of pinyon or a lonesome juniper the right size to pose by a cottage doorway.

It was tougher to keep to the traditional Ute trail across the Roan Plateau because, like himself and his steel-shod bay, the bare-hoofed Indian ponies hadn't been forced to follow a particular path across such wide open space and Ute were independent riders, even for Indians. But knowing where the trail *ought* to lead, and finding an ancient horse apple here, or a rusty trading post can there, Longarm was able to follow the drift to where, along about noon, he came to a more beaten path where the trail swung more to the west than he'd expected. So he followed it, muttering, "This ain't the way to that Green River Reserve. But what the hell, it sure leads *somewheres*."

So he rode on, and on, through most of the afternoon, breaking trail from time to time to refresh his mount from the water bag as he watched it go limp with nary a sign of a rain pond in sight.

Grazing his old cavalry vet on rabbitbrush as he consulted his survey map, Longarm confided, "If there's one thing meaner than any fickle woman it has to be fickle weather. Had that afternoon rain squall buckled down to really *water* this land, we'd have shallow ponds of bitty fairy shrimp all around us this afternoon. Since there ain't, we'd best get on down off this dry rimrock and back toward that river."

Mounting up again, he added, "Fuck where the Indians *used* to go along this particular trail. No Ute could be using her now unless they shop in Rangely these days!"

They rode on, and as if to prove his point, they ran out of plateau, and as they searched for a way down the far side, Longarm could see the smoke haze of Rangely rising from the silvery ribbon of the now not-too-distant White River.

They rode in well before suppertime. Longarm knew his mount was spent for the day and left her in the care of the town livery before he toted his saddle to the Western Union shed to send a mess of wires.

Then, having contacted everyone he wanted to after studying all day along on the range, Longarm asked about for a place to spend the night in Rangely.

There wasn't that grand a choice. Rangely was still little more than a wide spot on the trail to Utah Territory. An erstwhile Indian trading post now catered to the mostly prospecting crowd moving through the White River Valley. They said one old boy had filed a mining claim on an outcrop of *coal* he'd come across, for God's sake. Everybody knew it was tough to scratch a living out of high-grade ore when you found it out in the middle of nowheres much. Mineral wealth, from gold and silver down to coal and clay, sold where it was *needed,* at the going market prices posted on the Chicago or New York exchanges. Nobody was willing to pay you extra for your transportation costs. So *someday,* at a time the iron horse or at least some serious roads came through out Rangely way, there might just be some profit in the coal and oil shale some said they'd found along the bluffs north and south of town. But in the meantime they didn't seem to have a fucking *hotel* in Rangely.

Longarm griped some about that as he was enjoying a set-down supper of venison stew made with camus bulbs in a lean-to eatery run by a Señorita Conchita, she said.

When Longarm tried some of his border Mex on her, the pretty but sort of moon-faced dusky brunette looked thunderghasted, recovered, and told him she hadn't spoken the lingo since she was little.

Longarm let it go. He didn't ride for the army or the BIA. It was no never mind of his own if an English-speaking Ute gal wanted to pass herself off as a Mexican entitled to reside in Colorado.

He knew she was almost surely Ute the moment he tumbled to the fact she was Indian instead of Mexican. He knew she'd chosen to pass herself off as Mex because, like him, she'd known Ute looked more like Mexicans than most Rocky Mountain nations did.

This anthropology gal Longarm had known, in the Biblical sense by the time he'd got them out of all those cliff dwellings, had once told Longarm how most north-Mexicans and the far-flung wandering race of Uto-Aztec speakers appeared to have started out as one digger tribe in the Great Basin to the west and were more closely related to one another than they were to the taller Sioux-Hokan-, Iriquoian- or wide-ranging Algonquin-speaking nations. Something only Professor Darwin might have been able to explain had happened to the ancestors of the Uto-Aztec speakers, making them adaptable as hell as well as restless. One would never guess it just by looking at them, albeit they all shared a shorter more muscular build than say Cheyenne or Lakota, but the same original Indians had evoluted into nations as far apart and as different in custom as the bare-ass root-grubbing Paiute who'd never left their ancesteral range, the buffalo hunting Shoshone of the northern plains, the wild-ass Comanche of the southern plains, the civilized and peaceful Hopi of the southwest mesas and the civilized but bloodthirsty Aztecs of Old Mexico.

The old-time Spaniards having taught the Aztec subjects of His Most Catholic Majesty to wear pants and herd Hispano Moorish longhorns as the original "buckaroos" or vaqueros, the modern-day Mexican with enough Indian blood to matter tended to look more like Señorita Conchita trying to bullshit him in Colorado than *she* looked like, say, the Arapaho or Crow enemies of her kind. Longarm didn't care. He was facing a night on the range in his bedroll and it was starting to gray up in the west again. He said so as he washed down some of her Ute cooking with a fair imitation of *Taibo* coffee.

You could tell because a real Mex would have used some spice or at least more salt, and few newcomers to the mountain meadows dared to serve camus.

Camus bulbs were a tasty wild substitute for sweet onions, and a heap of folk, red or white, admired their taste. But when you didn't know what you were doing out this way and picked the *death camus* by mistake, you could wind up dead, or charged with the murder of a paying customer.

The two bulbs, like the two white wild mushrooms that could offer either a delicious meal or sure death within three days, no matter what they did for you, could be told apart easily enough by pickers who'd been taught from childhood how to do it. Longarm was leary about picking wild camus himself. But he figured an Indian gal would know better than to serve poison right on West Main Street. So he complimented her on her camus simmered in elk gravy.

She shot him a wary look, glanced about as if to make sure they were alone in her smokey lean-to and asked, "You know what they are? Most *Taibo*, I mean gringos, take them for sweet onions."

He smiled knowingly and replied, "Too sweet by half for onions. Had some baked in clay with some *Kwahadi* pals one time and . . ."

"You are Saltu ka Taibo!" she accused, wide-eyed, before she broke into a radiant smile and continued, "Real people told me you might be coming this way to hunt for *bad Taibo* for a change, and we thought this would be a good thing. We remembered how Saltu ka Taibo fought those bluecoats who were attacking the wrong band when Pia-Oha rose against Little Big Eyes in the South Pass country not too long ago. We knew you would not say any real people were stealing all those fucking cows when they were doing no such thing!"

Longarm asked if he could have more coffee. Indians lied as often as white folk, and he was still smarting about that blond sass on the palomino pony. He was neither flattered nor dismayed by the simple statement of fact his

Ute nickname stated. Saltu ka Taibo translated roughly as "stranger who is not a fucking son of a bitch," albeit some Indians held a *Taibo* was lower than any son of a bitch when they used it to designate a *white* stranger. Somewhere in the distance mountain thunder rolled. Longarm glanced out the open side of the lean-to where the sun still shone and sighed. "Like I was saying, I've been scouting for at least a dry hayloft if I can't find anyone who takes in boarders by the night, Señorita Conchita."

She laughed and said, "My real name is Connie Dancing Pony. We take our last names from our mother's side. My father was a mountain man and I am a Christian, or at least I don't believe that *Puha* bullshit. So I didn't want to move over beyond the Green River just because Nat Meeker was an asshole. A heap of us are still around, passing for something else or camped out where the *Taibo* dare not go because they are more afraid of heights. Why don't you shack up with me if you have nowhere to stay here in Rangely? Hear me, I am a Christian, sort of, and keep a clean cabin with no bugs in my bedding. Hear me, I take a bath once a month whether I need one or not and I have not slept with anybody for . . . Shit, going on eight weeks now!"

Longarm sipped thoughtfully as she silently waited, trying not to look as if she gave a shit either way.

Not wanting to be needlessly cruel, Longarm confessed, "That's more than *I* can say, Señorita Conchita. But I hope it's understood I am only passing through your fair city . . . ?"

She bitterly replied, "*City* my almost-Christian ass, and there's not a man in Rangely, save for Saltu ka Taibo, I'd even consider giving this child's ass to. So I'm clean and I shut down this cook-shack once the sun goes down. So would you rather carry me home or sleep out in the rain tonight, Saltu ka Taibo?"

To which Longarm could only reply, "Well, seeing you put it that way, Señorita Conchita. . . ."

Chapter 14

Connie Dancing Pony's pose as a possibly distantly related Mex mestiza fell apart the moment you entered her cozy well-kept cabin. It wasn't true Indians smelled worse than other folk. But they sure smelled *different* when they were going by the customs they'd been reared by. Aside from the different grub they et, most Indians, and Ute were Indian indeed, admired the smell of smoke and didn't mind smoke getting in their eyes half as much as white folk. Longarm knew Connie had been enjoying bare-ass upside-down smoke showers when she was alone and not pretending to be Mex. It gave a man who'd slept alone recently a tingle to picture anybody built like tawny Connie posing naked as a jay on spread legs above a smudge fire of smoldering sage and sweetgrass. In spite of her sweepings you could see where she'd been smoking her bare hide in the center of the dirt floor.

By that time they'd been flirting and smiling dirty at one another for close to a full hour. So when Connie barred her door and trimmed the lamp, hissing, "Hurry! I'm hot as a two-dollar pistol that needs reloading!" he commenced to undress in the dark, knowing she'd be at her less complexicated peasant blouse and wraparound skirts.

He fumbled his way in the dark to a deal table and piled his duds there, hanging on to his holstered six-gun as he asked her where she was so's they wouldn't crack heads getting into her sleeping pallet in one corner. She purred she'd catch him, and as he groped his way to join her, she caught him sure as hell by his dawning erection.

She gamely hung on as she gasped, "Have you been saving all of this for one poor lonesome Christian, sort of? Like Miss Mouse told the Froggie in that naughty song, this may not work but we can try!"

They tried and it worked. The chunky breed gal moaned in her old Momma's lingo as Longarm entered her tight, warm depths, convinced it was true she hadn't been getting any lately.

He'd sort of forgotten how swell it felt, as men were inclined to when they weren't at it night after night with the same gal until if they didn't watch out it could feel like *working*.

But as ever amid new surroundings, shoving his old organ grinder to a strange ring dang doo felt as if he'd just invented fucking for the first time, and from the way she was moaning and groaning as she moved in response to his thrusts, it seemed a new experience to Connie as well.

After they'd climaxed the way missionaries expected, Connie wanted to get on top, Indian style in spite of her new Mexican identity. Indian gals of all nations learned to be the one on top for the same reasons they followed their man single file along a trail, packing for the two of them whilst he kept his hands free for fighting and his eyes peeled for danger to them both. When folk were lacking in feather beds, a gal saved wear and tear on her tailbone by being the one on top. Indians were not inconsiderate as some white captive women said. They'd learned to live practical, closer to the earth. Old Chief Quinkent had insisted Arvilla Meeker would have never found it half as discomforting getting raped if she'd been willing to get on top like a natural woman.

They'd sent the sixty-year-old chief to prison for life without charging him with such an embarrassment for a white woman. Hanging him as the army wanted would have called for too much creative paperwork.

Connie came and kept coming with Longarm kissing her swell firm tits in turn. She giggled that his mustache tickled them. He never asked why she felt his mustache was such a novelty, and after he'd shot his wad up into her and it was time to cuddle and smoke their wind back, Connie murmured, "I'm glad I was too Christian, almost, to follow my mother's people across the Green River. My father's people are awfully mean, but that *Puha* chanting, with rattles and prayer sticks, is heap big shit, too!"

Longarm assumed she meant by that she didn't go along with the moral codes professed by Christian sky pilots. He found some of it sort of confining as well. But as they shared a smoke she suddenly blurted, "Why do us Christians always blame people for things they never did?"

He put the cheroot to her lush lips to reply, "Human nature, I reckon. Your mother's folk have some foolish notions about your dear old dad's folk. It aint true, for instance, that Indian children sent to BIA boarding schools are baked in ovens with apples in their poor little mouths."

She passed the smoke back and twiddled his dick as she insisted, "You blamed the Paiute for the Mountain Meadows Massacre, you blamed the South Cheyenne for the Hungate Massacre, and you blamed the Jews for killing Jesus Christ. Hear me, I have only met one member of the Jewish Nation and I didn't like him much. But I can read and I know the Jews could not have killed Jesus Christ if they'd wanted to."

Longarm blew a nostalgic smoke ring in the dark and confided, "I met this lady of the Hebrew persuasion, touring with a Wild West show as an Indian princess, come to study on it, who told me no Jewish courts would have been in session during the Jewish holy days you read of in the Good Book. She said that even had a Jewish court put Jesus to death they'd have never executed him Roman Style. When a Jewish court sentenced anyone to death, they were stoned or shoved off a cliff. She pointed out that our own scriptures say Jesus was nailed to that cross by Roman soldiers, too. But this parson I asked about that allowed the Romans did it to please the Jewish priests and old King Herod."

Connie gave his dick an impatient tweak and insisted, "Ain't that just like a lying *Taibo*? I read the *History of the Jewish Wars* by Josephus of Rome, a Jew living in Rome, writ about the same time as the New Testament and agreeing with it as to some details. But if the baby Jesus was born during the census of Caesar Augustus in the year of four B.C. as the Scriptures say, would you care to hear why Caesar Augustus had ordered them to *hold* that census?"

Longarm said, "I can hardly wait to hear. Would you let go of my poor old organ grinder or move your teasing hand faster?"

Connie moved her hand faster as she relentlessly went on, "They wanted a fresh tribal tally because King Herod had just up and *died*! King Herod never could have sent those wise men to find out what was going on in Bethlehem, nor ordered the slaughter of the innocents the Roman records fail to mention, because he died before Baby Jesus was born."

Longarm tried, "The Good Book likely refers to his son, the next King Herod, Junior."

Connie said, "Josephus says *his* name was Archelaus, and it doesn't matter because Josephus says that in six A.D., when Baby Jesus would have been around ten. The Romans gave up on the notion of running Judea as a reservation under a Jewish chief in favor of running it direct out of Rome through a Jewish Agency run by what they called a proconsul. So that's what Pontius Pilate was. He was running the Jew Reserve in twenty-nine A.D. when they brought Jesus of Nazareth before him on the charge of standing up to his appointed agent, the way our boys stood up to Nat Meeker that time!"

Interested in spite of himself, Longarm asked, "Then how come that reservation agent sent the prisoner before *somebody* the Good Book has down as King Herod?"

Connie said, "The Roman records don't say. Archelaus might have been living high on a Jewis Agency pension, the way you *Taibo* have Ouray on your leash of silver dollars, allowed to call himself a chief as long as he does what he's told by Washington. But the Romans had done away with Jewish puppet kings by the time Jesus was executed by the Roman in *charge,* the Proconsul Pontius Pilate, because Jesus or His followers kept proclaiming Him the savior of his nation and king of the Jews, promised before He was born by Elijah the Prophet, and *that* was why they crowned Him with a crown of thorns and stuck a sarcastic sign about beholding the King of the Jews above Him on the cross!"

Longarm snubbed out his cheroot to get a better grip on her as she went on gripping him, insisting, "Any *Jews* you asked on that reservation would have felt the notion of their own king just grand, even though most of 'em might have dismissed a holy man from out of town as some sort of harmless lunatic. It was the *Romans* He scared skinny with that talk about being born in the City of David to a momma descended from the Royal House of David!"

Longarm muttered, "I wasn't there!" as he rolled atop her to shove it where anything that stiff surely belonged.

But Connie was so wrapped up in her indignation that even as she moved her firm rump in response she moaned, "Neither was I. It was that other emperor I'm sort of named for who decided to blame it all on the Jews. He'd just decided Christian notions were easier to sell to his Romans than their old gods wearing fig leaves and fire engine helmets. So he pinned the death of Jesus on the Jews to ease Rome's guilty conscience!"

Longarm kept kissing whilst she tried to bust his back with her tawny thighs. But as he went limp atop her, with it throbbing softly as he soaked it in the afterglow, she said, as if nothing had just happened, "Why do people hug their guilty conscience to their breasts like some secret treasure? Why can't they just admit they did something wrong and get on with things?"

Longarm snorted, "Suffering snakes, I don't know! As a lawman I'm all too aware how dumb some folk can act when their conscience is gnawing at 'em. I mean to ask those bad girls how they feel about all the stock they've stolen once I catch 'em."

Then, as he calmed down enough to relight their cheroot for some quieter cuddling, Longarm mused, "That's something for *me* to gnaw on. Sometimes somebody with a guilty conscience behaves awfully odd, as if taunting others to catch them or mayhaps unable to stay away from the scene of a crime. Crooks are forever getting themselves in trouble by striding into a police station bold as brass to ask the desk officer how they're doing with such and such a robbery, or worse. I got to study on why one or more young gals would display themselves in broad day when it would be so easy to just lay low with the rest of their gang. We know they have to be riding with a gang. No two gals ever herded eighty or more head of range cows wherever in tarnations they've been herded!"

He got the cheroot going—it smelled better after it had burnt some—and told the Ute breed, "I want you to study on what comes next before you try to slicker me, Señorita Conchita. Neither the army nor the BIA has asked my advice on the current relocation of your momma's people. You say you don't like to see anybody blamed for anything they haven't done and that sounds reasonable. So let's see how my process of eliminating might work with the help of an expert on the subject."

She asked what he was talking about.

He said, "Them two bad white gals are scouting for Indian thieves or *Taibo* thieves. What can you tell me about Indians up to anything who may still be in these parts?"

She hesitated and asked, "You are speaking straight with me? What I say will not go to the Fifth Cav?"

He told he'd just said that.

Connie said, "Most, or all right many, of the real people are over in Utah Territory on land those Mormons thought they owned. Washington doesn't care what Mormons want either. Some real people still range where they have always ranged. Maybe not as close to the rivers. The hunting is much better with the land so empty. They don't need to hunt *Taibo* stock. There is plenty of deer, elk, bighorn in the high country now."

She thought and confided, "Many no longer listen to what Ouray the Arrow says about getting along with the *Taibo*. He is old and sick and the *Taibo* have tamed him with money in the bank, a fine log cabin and a beautiful young wife he is no longer man enough to fuck. Of the nine clans of my mother's nation, not all have been ordered to move across the Green River, and some bands of those who've agreed to go have not gone with them. Some of the young men who rode under Nicaagat and killed your major Thornburgh along the Milk River never surrendered and still hide their women and ponies in Coal

Canyon. Colorow and Quinkent surrendered and came in with many of the young men after that. But not *all*. Some still live the same old way among the head waters of the Piceance."

Longarm grimaced and said he'd have to take her word on that. He added, "I never saw a fresh horse apple when I passed through that lonesome valley earlier this very day!"

She sniffed and said, "You weren't supposed to. The Fifth Cav has rounded up all the real people who are *easy* to see!"

He laughed, kissed her, and after they'd smoked some, they made love some and even got some sleep as it commenced to rain fire and salt outside.

It rained well into the morning. So they lay slugabed, or *he* did, as Connie served him a swell breakfast in bed, of sage grouse eggs and store-bought bacon. When he commented, she said both red and white folk in those parts ate fresh game that cost next to nothing and only bought luxuries such as sardines, bacon, white flour and such as a change to go along with white sugar, coffee and whiskey. When he made mention of the Widow Ellison's butter and eggs trade over to the county seat, she sniffed and said they were city dudes who didn't know where to scout for free-for-the-taking wild food all around.

Longarm didn't argue. He knew she was both right and wrong. For Columbus had never discovered a Garden of Eden where innocent Adams and Eves roamed free, as peaceful noble savages.

Farming had been invented by earlier noble savages after someone noticed how *spread out* wild food grew "free-for-the-taking." You ran out of it sudden and took to braining one another over a venison haunch or a basket of acorns once you had more than one family foraging the area of a couple of townships, and so, had Columbus stayed put in Europe the hunting and gathering way of life would have still been doomed in just a few more generations of noble savagery.

Connie was a good sport when they parted, likely forever, around noon. Longarm sent more wires inspired by her revelations, toted his saddle back to the livery and forded the river to ride east along the north bank toward the county seat.

He took his time, canvassing other outfits without much luck until he got to the N Circle H late in the day, to find it buzzing like a bashed-in hornet's nest. When he asked what all the fuss was about, a wrangler declared, "We got hit last night in all that rain! The sneaks run off two hundred head we had pent to herd over to Fort Duchesne. They cut the wires and druv 'em through the downpour to erase every track and melt away every fresh cow pat for as far as the eye can see!"

Chapter 15

Big Newt Harper and most of his riders were out scouting for sign just the same. But the ramrod he'd left in charge, a likeable older cuss called Deacon Foss, had the Chinee whip up a Denver and some coffee for Longarm whilst he rested his ass and that army bay at last.

As they sat out back in that tent, Longarm told Deacon Foss about his near miss with that young gal across the river on that palomino.

Deacon Foss said, "By damn if we ain't spotted her on that same blond pony more than once! Albeit none of us have ever got close enough to jaw with her. On the south side of the river, you say?"

Longarm nodded, washed down some omelette and explained, "She was on a rise, posing to be seen some more from hereabouts. I threw her timing off first by riding shady down to the ford with all that willow and alder betwixt us. Then she failed to spot me fording the river until I was closer than she found comfortable, and of course she'd never counted on anyone chasing her cow pony with a cavalry mount."

Deacon Foss nodded knowingly and allowed, "I follow your drift. As many an Indian has learnt the hard way, a pony of Spanish Arab or Barb descent can beat a full-growed horse with Hanover or Trakehner cavalry lines hollow for the first quarter mile, but after that it ain't much of a contest. You say she reined in after she saw she'd never outrun you?"

Longarm said, "Bold as brass. Warned me she was a high-toned niece of the four Watson brothers, which later came as a surprise to the four Watson brothers. But she may have made a slip or more. I'll know better when I get back to Meeker. I wired old pals in other parts to look into some things for me and wire me back in care of Western Union at the county seat."

Deacon Foss naturally wanted to hear more. So Longarm explained, "The gal likely knew Watson was a Scotch name when she tacked another Scotch first name on to it. But the Watsons, knowing more about that subject than me, say she used the wrong sort of Scotch first name to go with their own. She was likely more scared than she was letting on and thinking fast. I'll be surprised as all get-out if she used her real name, but a gal who knew Watson was a Scotch name and grabbed yet another Scotch name out of thin air to go with it might not be a Greek or Romanian immigrant gal when you study on it. I know more than one Scot or Scotch-Irish American out this way. I've asked more than one for some helpsome hints on narrowing things down better. The Watsons suspect she might be of Highland Scot extracion. That narrows last names down considerable if ever I wind up with any Scots at all on my list of suspects."

Deacon Foss was sharp enough to ask, "You said she might have made more than one slip?"

Longarm nodded and said, "When she saw I expected her to ride home with her, she made up a visit to nobody at all on a nearby spread she named as the Hundred and Ten. We've already established there ain't no such brand in Colorado. But there's a One Hundred and *One* brand out California way, and who's to say where the sass came up with her own fictitious outfit on mighty short notice?"

Deacon Foss said he admired a man who could think on his feet, and invited Longarm and his jaded mount to spend the night.

It only took a moment's thought for Longarm to see Meeker would be there just the same if he rode in sensible. So he and his old army bay got a good night's rest and started out bright-eyed and bushy tailed in the morning.

It was just as well they had. Longarm stopped at a heap of spreads along the way to be served coffee, cake and gossip he couldn't really use, about neighbors of neighbors losing stock or spotting mysterious strangers riding sidesaddle in the distance. It seemed nobody else had gotten close as Longarm had to that one gal on the palomino.

The tedious day was nigh shot by the time Longarm approached Zelda Ellison's dairy farm from the west, with the sun about to set behind him. He'd have ridden by if the young widow and her two kids hadn't been out in the yard waving and hollering, as if it was important.

Longarm turned in to tick his hat brim and dismount as he asked the worried-looking Zelda what was eating her. She introduced the man of her house, the nine-year-old Hiram, who'd been in Meeker that afternoon. Zenobia told her big brother Longarm had been the one who'd taught her to spin a rope, so there. Zelda said to hush and ordered her boy to tell Longarm what he'd just heard in the county seat.

The nine year old told Longarm, "It's all over town. That old Bull Marlow is back on his feet with one arm in a cast, a belly full of redeye and his Walker Colt Conversion strapped on! He's been hunting high and he's been hunting low for the man who busted his arm and then knocked out half his teeth. Ain't you the man who did that to him?"

Longarm modestly confessed, "I reckon I am. It serves me right for not allowing him to bleed to death. I've been having a streak of such luck, lately."

Zelda Ellison said, "You have to stay here with us tonight. They say Bull Marlow has already shot out the windowpanes of your hotel room and told them at the livery that he'll burn them out if they don't tell him the moment you get back to town!"

Longarm smiled thinly and said, "All the more reason I can't put you and your children in peril, Miss Zelda. I might or might not meet up with the bully of your town before I ride on. But ride on I must, and should I somehow miss the grand opportunity for a rematch, you and yours will still be here and he might be even more dangerous once his right arm is out of that cast."

Hiram said, "They say he shoots left handed, mister."

Longarm soberly said, "Thanks for telling me, pard. I reckon I'd best get it on down the road now. I'm expecting some wires at that Western Union office."

Zelda said, "Custis, you can't ride in tonight with that fevered maniac on the lookout for you! I won't *let* you go to town tonight. You have to stay out here with us!"

He managed not to laugh. It wouldn't have been decent to observe he was more likely to "go to town" if he stayed out there with such a head turner. There were gals you talked to like so and were others it was best not to.

As he walked his bay toward the wagon trace, Zelda kept pace with him, leaving her kids behind as she pleaded in a more urgent tone, "Stay here tonight. I beg you. We've things to talk about, aside from Bull Marlow. I've been thinking about things we have to talk about ever since you . . . taught Zenobia how to spin a rope."

Out on the wagon trace in the gathering dusk he gently but firmly told her, "She's a sweet little gal. I like your boy, too, and to tell the pure truth I like you best of all, Miss Zelda. But I'd best be on my way now."

"What harm would it do for you to stay the night? Just one night?" she pleaded.

He said, "No harm at all to *me*. Mayhaps no harm to yourself, if I am following your drift. But long ago and far away in a mighty similar situation I found myself whittling whistles and making paper kites for a sweet little blue-eyed child who'd taken to calling me her uncle Custis. I swore I'd never let that happen again, because I know it hurt her more than it ever hurt her momma when the time came for her uncle Custis to ride on."

"Good heavens!" she flared. "Is that what you think I had in mind, you brute?"

So he said of course not, mounted up and rode on, hoping she'd stay good and sore a spell, lest those two kids wind up with memories of more uncles than any kids really needed.

When he rode into Meeker that night, he naturally stopped first at the livery to put his spent bay with the other, and when he saw the wary look in the stable boy's eye, he tipped him a whole quarter and said, "I heard. Go on and tell Bull Marlow I'm back. Where's he at right now?"

When the kid said the Last Chance, Longarm nodded and added, "Tell him I'll be by in an hour or so and save him the trouble of looking. Tell him I have some errands to run before we dance the hooly ann if that's his pleasure."

Then he toted his saddle over to the Medicine Horn. As he entered the lobby he told the unhappy-looking desk clerk, "I heard. The U.S. Government is fixing to pay for the new window glass because I'm on an expense account in the field. I won't be staying in my room up yonder before I settle this bullshit with Bull Marlow. So don't get your shit hot. I mean to store my saddle, grab a warm meal and see if I have any telegrams waiting for me at the Western Union before I do anything else. You can tell Bull that if he pesters you again."

He took his load upstairs, locked it away and came back down to ask if the hotel kitchen was still open. The worried-looking desk clerk said it had just closed. He might have been telling the truth. He might have just hated the sound of bullets hitting glass. Longarm asked in that case where he might treat himself to a set-down hot meal, explaining he was commencing to hate coffee and cake.

The clerk directed Longarm to a boardinghouse that served hot dinners to riders who didn't board there as late as nine or ten.

Longarm went first to the telegraph office, to find that nobody had wired back to him that early. As he was leaving, old Marshal Price caught up with him. Price said, "Longarm, I'm glad I got to you first! Bull Marlow's back on his feet and loaded for bear!"

Longarm said, "I heard. I don't reckon you'd care to hold him in durance vile until I was through here, even if I arrested the asshole for you?"

Price asked, "On what charge? How can I hold him if he ain't done nothing? Our justice of the peace would never issue me such a warrant. He's afraid of Bull Marlow, too."

Longarm shrugged and said, "It figures. I'm on my way over to that Miss Marlene Keller's boardinghouse and restaurant I've heard tell about. Is it worth the visit?"

Marshal Price seemed glad to change subjects as he replied, "Sure is! Miss Marlene serves swell spreads at reasonable prices. Order her High Dutch dumplings and that dish she makes . . . *Kalbfleisch* I think she calls it. Serves pilsner beer hauled over the Divide from that fancy brewery in Golden, too! Swell place to eat and, like I said, it ain't too steep."

So Longarm mosied on over to Fourth Street like they'd

told him to, and a young colored gal let him in to lead him to the dining room. Miss Marlene turned out a big rawboned blond woman of about fifty who'd have seemed a heap more motherly if she hadn't been wearing all that face paint and batting her Cleopatra eyes like so.

Longarm saw he'd showed up as the other four gents at the table big enough for a dozen were half-finished. Miss Marlene sat him down and leaned forward to rest her big tit on his shoulder as she asked him in a husky voice what he'd care to order.

Longarm said he'd heard swell things abut her pilsner, dumplings and . . . Kalomine?"

She laughed and said, "*Kalbfleisch.* Coming up. I promise you you'll like it. Everybody does."

To Longarm's surprise, since the pushy old gal made him feel like crossing his legs, the feed they put before him really hit the spot. A heap of High Dutch cooking was so close to plain old American you hardly noticed. The now nationwide "American Apple Pie" had started out High Dutch in Penn State, way back when. The dumplings boiled in a sort of broth, and what turned out to be breaded veal cutlets, tasted just different enough to make a man glad he'd ordered the same.

Dessert, served with swell coffee since he didn't want more beer with Bull Marlow on the prowl for him, consisted of a delicate many-layered pastry she called apple strudel. It was even sweeter than regular American apple pie. It was served with a slice of rat trap cheese. He pushed back from her table with the distinct impression he was never going to be hungry again.

Miss Marlene had mostly gushed over him whilst yet another older gal, of the colored persuasion, had been serving. The others, who'd all started earlier, had left the table by the time Longarm had his dessert. He was about to ask what he owed for such a swell meal when that younger colored gal called Miss Marlene out in the hall.

So Longarm smoked an after-supper smoke until the big old bovine temptress came back in with a worried look on her painted face, to say, "We're going to hide you 'way upstairs. We just got word from an earlier diner that Bull Marlow is headed down the middle of the street this way. He must have heard you were here!"

Longarm rose from the table to reach into his jeans as he replied in a less excited tone, "I'll see what he wants. How much do I owe you, Miss Marlene?"

She said, "Fifty cents but that's not important! What's important is that you're too young to die and sort of pretty! Why don't we just go upstairs and get to know each other better while my help sends him on a wild-goose chase? I've trained my girls to lie like rugs because a little white lie can save a lot of trouble when you're in the business of the care and feeding of cowboys!"

Longarm smiled at her, inspiring some eyelash fluttering indeed, and said, "I'd like to get to know you better, too, if I didn't have my reputation to worry about."

He caught the hurt look she shot his way and quickly added, "I'd be *proud* to have it known I'd carried on scandalsome with such a handsome gal if I didn't have more serious chores to tend, ma'am."

She blushed like a rose under all that paint and pleaded, "Don't go. Nobody's gonna fault you for avoiding a fight with the bully of the town. Everybody knows Bull Marlow's so crazy-mean you have to either kill him for keeps or just avoid him!"

Longarm said, "I know. I tried to settle our accounts the civilized way. But I've met the bully of the town in many a town, and whilst nine out of ten can be whupped to their senses, it's up to a sworn peace officer to deal with those nobody can reason with. So how would it look if word got around I'd refused to face a toothless drunk with a busted arm?"

Leaving sixty cents by his empty plate, Longarm circled the imposing presence of Miss Marlene to set his Stetson square and stride to and out her front door into the darkness of Fourth Street with a weary smile. When he saw nary a soul in sight, he strode out to the center of the street and started down it, loudly singing . . .

"I am looking for the bully,
The bully of your town,
I am looking for the bully,
But your bully can't be found!
So bring me out your bully,
And I'll lay him on the ground!
For I am looking for the bully,
The bully of your town!"

Chapter 16

Longarm meant well, but as that Scotch poet had warned, real swell plans of mice and men could go to hell in a hack, and when they put it all together later he would shudder to think how close he'd come to getting shot in the back.

Because what another of the townees so scared of him had told Bull Marlow at the Last Chance was that they'd seen Longarm walking up Fourth Street. Nobody had told Bull where he might be *going*. So by the time Longarm got out to the street Bull Marlow had passed by Miss Marlene's, striding sore and determined, in spite of a skin full of liquid courage, to be a city block and a half to the north as Longarm headed south, bellowing his taunting words.

Bull Marlow naturally heard and just as naturally turned around with a nasty toothless grin and a .45 Walker Colt Conversion in his still serviceable shooting hand.

But the first thing Longarm knew of all this came in the form of what sounded like a string of Chinee firecrackers or a double-action whore pistol going off behind him.

He naturally whirled for the darker shade along the

west side of Fourth as he drew his own .44–40. But the fusillade had occured too far off to have been aimed at *him*. So he eased up Fourth that way behind the trained muzzle of his six-gun.

He hadn't eased far when doors and windows ahead started popping open to spread streaks of lamplight back and forth across the dust of the unpaved street. A small crowd was already gathering around something sprawled in the dust at their feet. Longarm aimed his muzzle polite as he moved in to join them.

Town Marshal Price and Undersheriff Trumbo were already there, along with a younger lawman, wearing a copper star, and four townsmen. Two others joined them as Longarm got there. So it was to one of them that Price said, "Look what young Elmer Gibson just done, here! Shot it out man to man with the late Bull Marlow and kilt him with a Harrington and Richardson .32!"

A thin, sort of sissy-looking youth, in a suit and tie, modestly confessed, "I had to. It was him or me. You know how Bull could get when he was likkered up. I don't know why he was after me again tonight. I told him not to mess with me. But when he pointed that big hog leg right at me, I just did what I had to do!"

Another face in the crowd, having spotted Longarm, opined, "I can venture an educated guess as to what was eating old Bull, gents. He'd been saying earlier, more than once, he was looking for this deputy marshal from Denver with a view to his demise. Having failed to find him over this way, he decided to settle for what he could get when he met up with an old boy he'd pistol whupped in the past."

There came a murmur of agreement. Undersheriff Trumbo sniffed at the big .45 he'd picked up from the dust, cocked a brow and checked the wheel before he announced, "Bull's gun was empty! How come Bull was out looking to shoot Longarm, here, with an empty gun?"

The man who'd shot Bull Marlow said, "I didn't know his gun wasn't loaded! I thought he was fixing to fire it in my face when he swung it up like so! I'd have never shot him had I known he was only funning, and now I feel just awful!"

Marshal Price cocked a thoughtful brow to say, "I'll bet you do. He pistol whupped you with that same gun after he'd shot up the ceiling of the Last Chance last March as I recall. So where were you earlier this evening, Elmer? Were you by any chance bellied up to the bar with the rest of Bull's ass kissers when he declared he meant to clean a lawman's plow with that pissoliver he brandished and carried so casual?"

Elmer defensively replied, "I may have been down to the Last Chance earlier. Everyone knows I generally stop by for a drink or more after work. Just what might you be implying, Dad Price?"

An older, more authoritive voice in the crowd chimed in, "Dad ain't implying shit, Elmer. We all know Bull Marlow was a pain in the ass a heap of us wanted shed of, fair, square or who gives a shit, and Dad knows it's an election year. Don't you, Dad?"

Marshal Price shot Undersheriff Trumbo a thoughtful glance. Trumbo shrugged and said, "Your call, Dad. *I* don't want it on a silver plate!"

Marshal Price said, "Doc Prentiss, our elected coroner, will no doubt find it was a simple case of self-defense on the part of young Elmer here. The late Bull Marlow had declared he was out to kill somebody this evening, and it wasn't Elmer's fault Bull forgot to load his gun, or let somebody at the Last Chance empty it on him earlier."

There came a collective growling of agreement from the gathering crowd. Somebody said the occasion called for a drink. Marshal Price told his kid deputy not to abandon the body before Doc Prentiss sent a litter for it and said to tell the coroner they'd find him over at the Last Chance if they needed him later.

Longarm was more than willing to go along. For once he didn't even have to sign a deposition, and he still had some eliminating to do. Elmer Gibson was more than welcome to the dubious fame of being known as the man who'd shot Bull Marlow. Longarm wished the wishy-washy priss luck in living up to his legend even if he had pulled a sneaky trick on a bully who'd once humiliated him.

Longarm studied on the theme of revenge as he hung back just taking the scene in, and it slowly sunk in to young Elmer that the man he'd no doubt killed a thousand dirtier ways in his tormented mind would never scare him so bad again. It was a caution how it never occurred to the bully breed that the weaker creatures they kept torturing might nurse grudges long after the fun wore off. What had been the name of that one bigger kid at the old schoolhouse back in West-By-God-Virginia?

Rabbit. That had been what they'd called that kid with buckteeth, a head taller than any other kid in school, or most of their parents.

As a smaller boy, Longarm had tried high and he'd tried low to avoid a fight with old Rabbit, until the day finally came, out in the schoolyard, with big old Rabbit waiting and no way to get home but through him. So a then way smaller Custis Long had just gone through him, swinging and missing half the time and getting hit, hard, more than once, until all of a sudden the bigger kid was running away all a-blubber, with his dirty hands to his bleeding nose, whilst everybody slapped the winner on the back and pretty Peggy Jergens said he was braver than young David in the Good Book because he didn't need no *rocks* to hit any big bully with!

As they entered the saloon, Longarm could have told Elmer Gibson what would have happened to Bull Marlow had he lived. The fact Elmer had screwed up the nerve after watching Bully get the shit kicked out of him the other night bespoke the fate about to befall the bully of their town.

Back home in West-By-God-Virginia Larry Riggins had been the first of the other kids to hang a right cross on Rabbit's nose before it had time to heal, and after Rabbit missed the whole afternoon in school, the girls had assured Larry Riggins he was a hero, too.

So then Timmy Alcott had coldcocked old Rabbit in the cloakroom and Jack Jenkins rabbit punched him seated at his desk, until in the end his folk had taken him out of school and either moved away or let him grow up ignorant. Nobody back home could say for certain. Being a champion bully didn't get you anything but the sincere dislike of most and the bitter burning thirst for revenge only a sissy could feel.

Having drunk to the new bully of the town, Longarm set out to do some more eliminating. Recognizing one of the other diners from Miss Marlene's, Longarm drifted over to remark on wishing he'd saved more room for suds. The shorter man, who said they called him Jake, agreed Miss Marlene put on a swell feed for four bits and allowed he roomed with her as well.

Longarm said, "I've been staying at the hotel. Been thinking about a boardinghouse if I'm stuck here much longer. I know what your Miss Marlene has to offer. They say there's another lady called Helena Gorse as hires rooms to strangers just passing through?"

Jake said, "You don't want to board there. Miss Helena's all right, I reckon, but she runs a butcher shop out front and they slaughter at times in the backyard. Lord knows why some few cowhands stay upstairs there when they come to town. But they do. So she must charge less than anyone else, or fuck cheaper."

He sipped some suds, reconsidered and confessed,

"That was a low remark to make about any woman you don't know well enough to say that about. So forget I said it. I just don't know what she charges riders to board above her butcher shop."

Longarm said, "I understand this Helena Gorse had a cowboy called Slender Sam boarding with her before she commended him to a job on a dairy farm outside of town?"

Jake said, "Never heard of him. Hold on, are we talking about a tall drink of water who just got out of Canyon City?"

When Longarm said they might be, Jake said, "He et with us over at Miss Marlene's a time or two. Can't say why. They say old Helena Gorse serves steak and potatoes three times a day. They say Slender Sam did time for stealing stock. Don't know if that's true. But when you ain't certain you don't hire. I understand he got laid off out to Zelda Ellison. Last I heard he'd told everyone he was bound for the Sweetwater country up Wyoming way."

Longarm said that was about what he'd heard and changed the subject to those mysterious bad girls everyone had been talking about.

Jake said working in town as a blacksmith he heard all the local gossip but seldom got out on the range to meet up with mystery gals.

Longarm nodded, almost letting that get by him. Then he brightened and asked, "Hold on, Jake. Would you know just how many others there might be shoeing horseflesh in these parts?"

Jake said, "Sure I would, if I had any competition to worry about. But I'm it. You need a pony shod you bring him to me, and like that mess sergeant said, if you can't stand my cooking join the other side!"

Longarm signaled that vapidly pretty barmaid to put fresh heads on both their schooners and told the only blacksmith for miles, "The reason I suddenly find you so interesting is that you'd be the one either of those mysterious bad girls would come to if they needed a blacksmith. We're talking in at least one case about a right pretty teenager with long straight hair that matches the tail of her palomino. She rides it with a braided buckskin quirt, no hat, in a light tan whipcord habit on a Venus Brand sidesaddle?"

Jake said, "I'm way ahead of you on that palomino. I ain't shod one palomino since I set up shop here in Meeker. Have you asked old Fred Cooper downstream in Rangely? He's the only other cuss in the business here in Rio Blanco County, far as I know."

Longarm said, "I wish I'd considered that elimination when I was over that way. I can ask the sheriff's department here at the county seat to question him for me. It's only a long shot. I'm betting neither of those bad girls have their ponies shod in Rio Blanco County."

"Where else would a Rio Blanco County rider take their fool mounts to be shod, then?" Jake demanded, adding, "You can run out of horse all at once if you don't see to their hooves regular, you know!"

Longarm said, "Cavalry mounts are reshod once a month. Cow pony may go six or eight weeks without a visit to the smith if the wrangler has an eye for raised clinches or cracks. I somehow suspect those bad girls are riding well-shod mounts a long way from home."

The blacksmith said, "No hoof, no horse. I follow your drift. If they ain't from around here they have to be long-riding in and out from some other range. Utah Territory? What if they're thieving Mormon gals?"

Longarm said, "I've wired Fort Duchesne and the Salt Lake Temple. I've wired Grand Junction and some old pals up Wyoming way. So like the old church song says, farther along we'll know more about it. I sincerely hope."

A familiar voice from behind him asked what he was

hoping he'd find out by wiring high and low about those bad girls.

Longarm turned to nod at big Newt Harper and say, "Evening. Did you come over to the county seat to file another complaint? I heard as I passed through about your N Circle H getting hit again."

Newt Harper looked worried as he nodded grimly and replied, "Hit us hard and dirty in that driving rain! Ran off half the beef I had left and never left us a lick of sign. What was that you were just saying about wiring lawmen in other parts?"

Longarm shook his head and said, "Not lawmen. Old pals in the beef industry. Lawmen in all directions have been asked to watch out for missing cows. Cattle folk know more about the topic, and as your own ramrod must have told you I told him, that one young sidesaddle snip I got close enough to swap fibs with may have made a couple of slips. I'll know better after I get answers to wires I sent earlier up to the Sweetwater country."

Newt Harper gasped, "Are you saying you suspect them thieves have been running my stolen cows back up around them railyards where I got 'em to begin with?"

Longarm said, "Too early to say for certain. But can you think of a better place to sell your beef than where you bought it to begin with?"

Chapter 17

Big Newt Harper and Jake the blacksmith exchanged stricken looks and exclaimed as one, "The Union Pacific Railroad!"

Newt Harper added, "Of course! Why didn't we think of that? It's the only sudden way out of this high country for days on the trail in any direction! The U.P. Line runs through the South Pass grasslands going lickety-split but stopping half a dozen times along Bitter Creek before it crosses the Divide sweet and low for the hungry East! But all the stock they've run off carries Colorado brands and . . . Oh, shit, I follow your drift!"

Longarm said, "When I stopped by the Lazy Four to ask about that Hundred and Ten brand, the Watsons consulted a Colorado register. Your average Wyoming lawman would have a *Wyoming* register handy, and whilst it's true there's a government all-points out on beef branded N Circle H, a local outfit with a similar brand and a good local rep wouldn't find it impossible to poke cows aboard at dawn or in the tricky light of sundown, C.O.D. to Omaha or even Chicago. Nobody at the slaughterhouses at the end of the line pays attention to the brands as they skin out an honestly acquired carcass."

He finished his beer and added, "Meanwhile I'm just baying at the moon until I get some answers to them wires I mentioned. So as long as I'm waiting I may as well eliminate some more."

Newt Harper volunteered to tag along and help if Longarm was out to arrest anybody.

Longarm shook his head and said, "May not need to arrest nobody if this particular loose end dangles the way I suspect it might. I'm just out to make sure we understand how much beef has been pilfered by petty thieves and how much has been stolen serious."

Newt Harper said, "Only take a hard rider four or five days to get on up to the cross-country rails. Those crooks who hit us in that rain last night won't get half that far in four days, driving longhorns over hill and dale!"

Longarm nodded but said, "The question before the house ain't how *far* they've gone, Newt. It's which way they *went*. Since I first started riding for Marshal Billy Vail six or eight years ago I've learned to respect his knack of tracking outlaws on paper, setting at his desk like a fat old tabby by a mouse hole. It ain't as much fun as riding the range in circles. But it can sure save you some riding when you track down the home address of an owlhoot rider on paper."

He saw neither older man seemed to be following his drift. He told them, "Just guessing which way they're driving all that beef on the hoof can ride a man's ass half off as he tries to cover every base. But when and if he has some notion where they're headed, it's duck soup simple to head off a herd of cows when you're riding a cavalry mount!"

As he headed out the door, that vapidly pretty barmaid called out something about quitting time and Newt Harper said he meant to ride with Longarm as soon as he knew where they'd meet up with those damned cow thieves and his cows. Newt bitched they'd come close to ruining him.

He said another such raid would have him in debtor's court and added, "I got riders who got to be paid before I pay any other bills, and I'm way in arrears of some purchases already!"

Longarm didn't argue. He said he'd let Newt know as soon as he found out anything about his missing stock. He knew how much tougher it was to become a cattle baron than it was to dream about it. That was one reason he was a lawman instead.

Just dreaming, it seemed easy enough to file a homestead claim on a well-watered and wooded quarter section surrounded by open range. Logs in high country, sods in prairie country or 'dobe in drier country were there for the taking if you had the strong back and weak minds to build a home spread, and once you had that set up, all you had to do was stock it. That was where the ante got steeper. Ten-dollar scrub calves could be reared in three or four years to beef on the hoof selling for forty dollars a head in Omaha or sixty dollars a head in New York City.

When you culled out the best she-calves for breeding stock and mayhaps paid for the services of a prize beef bull, you could upgrade as well as increase your herd for little more than your labor costs on free grass and water, Lord willing and you didn't get hit by Indians, stock thieves or grasshoppers before the westward ho of fenced-in rival homestead claims pushed you farther west. But gathering your first scrub stock with money on the barrelhead before they gained a pound was a harder row to hoe than it looked. You had to start out rich or saddle yourself with at least a five-figure debt before you could hope to turn your first profit. Most cattle outfits never turned a profit before they'd survived those five summers it took to prove your home spread water rights and such. That "Code of the West" bullshit old Ned Buntline wrote about them stringing cow thieves up when they caught 'em with a running iron on 'em wasn't inspired by romantical notions of a horseback tradition. It was a matter of desperate measures by men who just couldn't survive such losses. A cattle baron who went broke was a cowboy looking for a job and owing more money than he'd ever in his life be able to pay back.

By the time Longarm retraced his steps to Miss Marlene's boardinghouse it was well past ten. He apologized to the young colored gal who came to the front door, and he said, "I ain't here social. I'm here in my officious capacity as an officer of the law."

She showed him into their front parlor and said she'd fetch Miss Marlene. Longarm was standing by the bookcase, trying to make out some of the titles printed in old-timey lettering, when Miss Marlene came in with her hair unbound, in a rose chenille robe over her nightgown, he assumed. She said her girl would fetch them hot chocolate and waved him to a love seat as she said, "We heard about Elmer Gibson shooting Bull Marlow. Who'd have ever thought Elmer had it in him, and to what might I owe this unexpected pleasure . . . Custis?"

He said, "I'm eliminating, ma'am. No offense, but the titles of more than one of your nicely bound books match up with your last name and the menu of those swell meals you serve in the back."

She sat down beside him, the fit of both their rumps on that love seat sort of snug, to reply, "I was born to Bavarian parents in Texas and raised to speak both languages about as easily. Do you find that *suspicious* for heaven's sake?"

Longarm said, "Not hardly. I said I was eliminating. I *have* some suspicions about an ex-convict they call Slender Sam Schneider. Am I correct about his name being a High Dutch name, Miss Marlene?"

She nodded and said, "Of course. It would translate as Tailor. I know the kid. He stayed for supper more than once after making a delivery. What about him, Custis?"

Longarm said, "Eliminating. I might have guessed before I studied harder that *Kalbfleisch* sounded a heap like Calf Flesh because that swell meal you served tonight was mighty tender young *veal* and most economy meals in these parts seem to consist of wild game, ma'am."

The colored gal came in with a tray holding hot chocolate and more Vienna pastries. As she set it before them on a low-slung rosewood table, Miss Marlene said, "Thank you, Willa. Would you be kind enough to tell Deputy Long, here, where we got that veal we've been serving this week?"

The serving girl looked confused and said, "Yes'm. We got that side of veal off Miz Gorse the butcher lady, same as before."

The big rawboned blond thanked her and sent her on her way. As she poured hot chocolate she asked Longarm if he wanted to examine what was left of her purchase, hanging in her ice chest in the basement.

Longarm shook his head and said, "Makes more sense if I take your word, Miss Marlene. The Widow Ellison as much as accused Slender Sam Schneider of stealing two veal calves from her. She told me she hired him on the commendation of Helena Gorse, and you and your serving girl ain't the only ones who've identified her as a butcher, slaughtering and vending meat whilst Slender Sam was boarding with her. It eliminates down to a two-faced churchgoer sending a boarder with an admitted criminal record to steal stock in the dead of the night."

He had no call to pull away from her fleshy knee draped over his own as he added, "There was saloon talk about Miss Helena and the saddle tramps she boards above her butcher shop. Starting to remind me of a trash woman called Belle Starr, over to Younger's Bend in the Indian Territory."

The possibly more refined landlady on the love seat

with him asked in an anxious voice if he'd heard any saloon talk about herself.

He honestly answered, "Not hardly, ma'am. Word about a lady's private life don't wind up in saloons when she's halfway . . . discreetable."

She snuggled closer, an almost frightening thing to contemplate, as she asked just how he defined the word "discreet."

He said Queen Elizabeth had defined it as not scaring the horses in the streets, whilst Queen Victoria had allowed she didn't care what her ladies in waiting did as long as she never heard about it.

Miss Marlene said in that case she'd be obliged if he'd carry the tray whilst she led the way to more discreet surroundings. He was too polite to repeat that remark Ben Franklin had made about older women. But it did seem true they didn't yell, they didn't tell and they were grateful as hell. Albeit once they got to it up in her bedchamber she moaned loud enough in High Dutch about him committing "Octopus on my liver" as near as he could make out.

He wasn't all that concerned with what she might be *saying* as she tried to give birth to him in reverse with her big wet hungry love maw and her long milk-white limbs wrapped around him. The contrast betwixt such a big old literally white woman and the tawny Connie the night before made up for some of the time might have flown under old Marlene's bridges since she'd been firmer of flesh all over. As variety, there was something to be said for a big rawboned figure with its big bones wrapped in marshmallow. So when her false-teeth slipped as he was kissing her and he never said anything, she commenced to cry. He didn't ask why. He kissed her some more and pounded harder whilst she kept moaning about him being her liver socks, whatever that meant.

After he'd made her come, she asked him to trim the

bedlamp, and when he started to light a cheroot in the dark, she asked him not to, confessing, "I'm still blushing like a schoolgirl, *mein liebe! Gott* knows I'm no schoolgirl and that was so gallant of you not to laugh. So let's talk about that veal downstairs while I recover my poise! I've been trying in vain to see how the meal I served you earlier has anything to do with . . . this."

He snuggled her closer, absently wondering just where he'd last seen his duds as he reached out in the dark to determine his six-gun hung from the bedpost after all. He said, "I'll tell Marshal Price in the morning and he can handle Helena Gorse's petty thievery as he sees fit. If it was up to me I'd let her off with a warning after she made restitution. I'm sure the Widow Ellison and others missing a few head would rather have the money than see her doing time. She's no danger when she can't find boyfriends to steal stock for her, and once Dad Price has his eye on her, she'll have a time getting away with it again."

Marlene said, "Oh, from the way you were talking downstairs I thought it was more important."

He said, "It *was* important until I *eliminated* it. I've been trying to form a pattern in my mind, and now that I see some if not all the smaller losses were the work of *other* thieves, the pattern's a whole lot clearer. There's more to all this razzle-dazzle than simple theft!"

She hadn't been listening. She murmured in a little-girl-lost tone, "We were poor when I was little and my momma fed me white bread and jam till all my baby teeth were rotten and my second teeth came in as bad. I haven't had any teeth at all since I was twenty-five and, oh, Custis, I thought I'd die when my plate slipped like that whilst we were fucking!"

He patted her robust shoulder soothingly and said, "It's tough for folk to keep such secrets once they get so . . . informal. They say no man is an Adonis to his valet, and I've often suspected some of you great beauties are more worried about us catching you with your paint and corsets off than you're worried about your ring dang doos. But, hell, everybody in this world burps and farts and sometimes throws up or shits themselves. Letting others in on the fact we're all mushy and wet inside is the price we pay unless we want to live celibrated in an airtight box. Nobody's teeth are perfect and you ain't the first gal I ever met with false teeth. I met this opera singer one time who had neither teeth nor a hair on her head and she was still pretty enough to star at the Tabor Opera House in Leadville."

"Did you fuck her?" Marlene laughed, dirty as all get-out.

Not knowing which way might work best, he sedately said he never gossiped about such matters. She took the matter in hand and confided in a downright dirty tone, "I'm glad. There's something I've been dying to try since I was twenty-five. But I've always been so ashamed and afraid they'd tell, or, worse yet, laugh at me!"

Longarm said he was game for most anything that didn't hurt but added on a cautionary note, "The Chinee say to be careful what you wish for lest you get it, and without naming names, I'd better warn you about this gal I met who'd found a paperbound copy of the Kama Sutra and wanted to try something that threw her back out in the end."

Marlene purred, "Just lie still. Don't say a word while I get sort of dirty with you!"

So he did as she said, and as she kissed her way down his belly in the dark, it kept getting harder and harder, until all of a sudden she had it in her toothless mouth and it was all he could do to keep from blurting that felt even better there in Meeker than it had in Leadville.

Chapter 18

Longarm read his wires on the Western Union steps in the morning sunlight, nodded, and toted his saddle over to the livery. He asked them to saddle the bay he hadn't ridden since he'd made it to the county seat, and then dropped next door to the general store to stock up on trail supplies and an X-frame pack saddle. He led both mounts on foot over to jaw first with Dad Price and then across the way at the courthouse.

The town marshal allowed he'd handle the matter of Helena's underselling wild venison with prime veal the way that might hurt her most and save the county the cost of a trial. At the courthouse across the way Longarm found the county sheriff was still off kissing babies in an election year, with Undersheriff Trumbo still in the catbird seat.

When he said he'd gotten answers to some wires he'd sent earlier, Trumbo said, "I got some, too. You first."

Longarm said, "Can't prove nothing yet. Don't see how else things eliminate as well. There *is* a Hundred and Ten brand, registered in Wyoming Territory. Better yet, the spread's in the Bitter Creek stretch of the Sweetwater country."

Trumbo handed Longarm a cigar and grinned, "You

said you suspected that sass on the palomino didn't have time to study as she was trying to pull the wool over your eyes, bold as brass and scared skinny. So she and her gang have at least passed through the range to the north, right?"

Longarm bit the end off the cigar. It was a nickel brand but still smelled better than those more expensive stinkers old Billy Vail blew in his poor face down Denver way.

Thumbnailing a light for the both of them, Longarm went on to say, "Like I said, I still got to *prove* all this. But the Hundred and Ten brand is registered to a young widow Menzies, maiden name MacAlpin, and her kid sister, Una MacAlpin, as an equal partner. The older sister's first name is Elsbeth. We're talking about ladies of Highland Scotch descent, like the Watsons warned me."

Trumbo took the cigar from his lips to whistle and say, "Hot damn, let's posse up!"

Longarm shook his head and replied, "Let's not and say we did. I'm riding alone up yonder because to begin with my jurisdiction extends across county and even state lines whilst yours doesn't, and after that I could still be full of shit. You got to catch a thief with the goods before you can make an educated guess stick. The Menzies-MacAlpin gals ship beef east from the stop at Thayer Junction on Bitter Creek, by way of the Union Pacific when folk are watching. Trying to think like a cow thief driving purloined beef from these parts to market on the sly, I'd surely load 'em aboard a night train somewheres *else,* albeit in some cow town where I was known as a more honest cuss. My survey map tells me I'd want to aim for Rock Springs, east of the Flaming Gorges but west of the salt wells that give Bitter Creek its name. I know the country. Far east as the *town* of Bitter Creek, Bitter Creek runs sweet as the rest of the sweetwater in the Sweetwater country."

Longarm took a drag on the cigar and said, "The bigger stop up at Rock Springs lies along the saltier Bitter Creek downstream. But they get their water, plenty of water, from them nearby rock springs, along with a creek from the north partly fed by Reliance Springs. So they have a shithouse full of holding and loading pens yonder, and once you get beef close packed betwixt corral poles, after driving 'em in around sundown or sunrise . . ."

"You sure I can't come with you?" Trumbo sighed.

Longarm said, "Nope. Waste of time if I'm wrong. I'll hold back and recruit some Wyoming lawmen if I'm right. Don't have to move in on 'em before they get to Rock Springs, if that's where they're headed. You say you got something on the wire as well?"

Trumbo said, "I sure did. Don't see what it means, though. They had this big shoot-out down in Glenwood Springs and now they've sent out an all-points on the sole survivor. Seems a surly cuss from Hot Sulphur Springs led his clan into a knock-down-drag-out with the notorious Tracy Twins, Pat and Mike, down along the Colorado."

Longarm said, "Heard of the Tracy Twins. Guns for hire. Said to be sneaky as well as mean."

Trumbo said, "So the Tarringtons found out. Took some time to add it up so, but, having fought his way through the Tarringtons, Pat Tracy sent a gal to claim his dead partner's body and ship it to Denver for him. They didn't really have nothing on her that would stick. But being a doxie with a long yellow sheet she didn't know that. So they sweat the story out of her. Seems Pat and Mike were out our way to murder somebody for a Denver boss the gal couldn't name, when they tangled with the Tarringtons by mistake."

Longarm said that was all mighty interesting but . . .

"The one Pat and Mike Tracy had been sent out our way to kill was *you,* Longarm," the local lawman cut in.

Longarm took a long thoughtful drag on the cigar before he sighed and said, "Shit. Just as I thought I had it all figured out! I can't make *that* piece fit worth shit! Do they offer a description of this remaining Tracy Twin, Ford? I've never laid eyes on either and none of the flyers I've read on 'em agree on what they look like."

Waterford Trumbo said, "The dead one describes as short and mighty muscular. Gal says Pat's taller, leaner and if anything meaner. She says Pat hired her to gather the remains in Glenwood Springs and ship 'em to a Denver undertaker. They didn't converse in depth in Lyons, where she was dealing in stolen goods before her arrest."

Longarm scowled and said, "That makes even less sense if they were after this child! Maybe Pat Tracy lost track of me down south and now he's waiting on the far side of the Divide for some backup. Maybe if the dog hadn't stopped to shit it would have caught the rabbit. So I reckon I'll be going now."

Ford Trumbo walked him out front, where they shook on it and Longarm mounted up to do some more serious riding.

He chose a traditional Ute pony trace the army had down as fairly direct for Wyoming Territory, since getting there first sounded way easier than fighting the Menzies-MacAlpin sisters and their trail hands along the way. The recently opened Colorado range was barely settled along the bottomlands of the east-west river, so he soon had the rolling Danforth Hills and their lonesome pinyons all to himself.

Swapping mounts as he broke trail once an hour, walking 'em up and trotting 'em down, he made the headwaters of the north-flowing Milk River before noon and followed it on down to the wider, albeit not that much wider, Yampa, where as expected, the traditional trail led to an easy ford across brawling whitewater. But by then the day and his ponies were about worn out, so when he came upon yet another of those saucer-shaped outcrops with a limpid pool of rainwater full of fairy shrimp in the middle, he told his spent ponies, "This must be the place," and dismounted to make camp for the night.

First things coming first, Longarm led the old army bays just outside the natural bowl to tether them in a growth of cottonwood after he'd watered them good and fed them some store-bought oats, whilst he peeled them barebacked and rubbed them down with an empty feed sack. He told them he'd be back with nose bags of rainwater before he turned in for the night, and moved back inside the natural fort to see to his own comforts. He spread his bedding on higher and drier pea gravel over where the bedrock parted company with it, broke out some canned grub and turned his saddle upside down to dry. He'd just gathered some dry grass and windfall when a familiar voice rang out. "Hello the camp! Is that you in yonder, Longarm?"

It was big Newt Harper, setting his lathered pony next to one of his hands, a kid he introduced as Tony. Tony and his pony looked as lathered. Longarm said, "Howdy. I see you boys talked to Ford Trumbo behind my back. You look like you've both been chased all day by dog soldiers or worse."

As they dismounted, Newt Harper said, "I asked you to let us in on it as soon as you found out anything, dammit. What's all this about the MacAlpin sisters and my cows?"

Longarm moved to drop his load of tinder and firewood betwixt his bedding and the rain pool as he replied, "I told Ford Trumbo I wasn't ready to press any charges. Guessing is one thing. Proving is another. You know these MacAlpin sisters, Newt?"

The burly cattle baron said, "Not as cow thieves. Dealers. They buy and sell beef on the hoof up along Bitter Creek. Their home spread would be . . . let me see . . ."

"Thayer Junction, Boss," young Tony cut in, adding, "They're purdy."

Newt Harper nodded and said, "That's it. Thayer Junction. I think they brand beef they raise with a Hundred and Ten, now that I study on it, feeling dumb. Being dealers they poke heaps of critters aboard the U.P. cattle cars wearing their original brands and . . . Jesus H. Christ! Why has it taken me this long to see what you seem to be seeing, Longarm?"

The younger lawman who'd just got there modestly replied, "They pay me to puzzle out such patterns. You and the others down along the river had no way of knowing your stock was being run north to Wyoming instead of many another way, and after that you naturally took it for granted your stock was being run off by sneaky neighbors or somebody none of you didn't know from long ago and far away. So it never occured to any of you to consider a more distant outfit that *knew* where all your unfenced stock would be grazing, lightly guarded and ripe for the taking if the taker had a handy means of moving it clean out of cattle country in their own hired boxcars!"

Newt Harper swore and muttered something dirty about two-faced, double-dealing redheads. That was the first indication Longarm had that the older sister might not be another blonde. Young Tony gushed. "You can say that again, Boss! As I recall them MacAlpin sisters *sold* you some of them cows they just stole back from you!"

His boss nodded grimly and said, "We're all going up yonder, come the cold gray dawn, for a full accounting! Come on, Tony, let's you and me tether our own mounts over in them cottonwoods with Longarm's before we spend some time around the campfire plotting their impending trial! Longarm here is right about you needing proof to put a cow thief away, even when they can't offer to fuck their way out of it!"

Longarm hunkered down to pile windfall on his tinder as the two of them led their cow ponies out of his sight. He'd just struck a light when a shot rang out, and as Longarm rose to his full considerable height Newt Harper came running back, six-gun in hand, yelling at Longarm to take cover and adding, "They're all around us! They got us pent in this fucking saucer like kitchen roaches caught at the cat's milk! They got Tony! I fear he's dead! You cover the north rim whilst I try to hold this south side."

Longarm drew his .44–40 with a sober nod of understanding. But instead of turning his back on such a pal, he said, "I'd be obliged if you was to drop that gun and grab for some sky, Newton Harper!"

The already flushed stockman tried swinging the muzzle of his own gun rudely. Longarm fired first. Harper's treacherous six-gun went off, but his round flew wild as two hundred grains of hot lead backed by forty grains of black powder pushed him off his feet to set him on his ass in the rain pool.

Longarm muttered, "Shit, I was fixing to *use* that water!" and moved fast to grab one of Harper's booted ankles with his free hand and haul the dying man out atop dry gravel before he could piss his pants, as they were so inclined.

Spread sprawly as a carelessly kicked bearskin rug at Longarm's feet, Newt Harper stared up and through the younger man who'd just killed him, to marvel in a weak voice of wonder, "How did you know? Who told you?"

Longarm reloaded as he soberly replied, "You did, Newt. Never say someone else fired the only shot to be heard in recent memory with your own gun still *smoking* in your hand. Hold the thought. I got to see if Tony might still be saved."

His own gun still in hand, since he still had some loose ends all adangle, Longarm legged it out of the bowl and over toward their four tethered mounts, to find young Tony facedown in the grass with a little hole drilled through the back of his skull and half his face blown away when you turned him over.

Longarm holstered his six-gun, saying, "I'm sorry as hell, but now I'm sure the two-faced treacherous bastard was keeping all his hands in the dark as well. Saves us a heap of arrest warrants, Tony. Just lay still here whilst I see if I can get anything else out of your boss."

He couldn't. When he hunkered down by the one he'd shot, Newt Harper had breathed his last to just lay there grinning like a shit-eating dog.

Longarm told him, "Aw, you wasn't all that clever, you cheap bastard. Had you been half as smart as me you'd have figured out who was raiding your herd long before I did. Instead of complaining to the War Department and BIA you could have dealt with those MacAlpin gals in private and your Uncle Sam never would have sent this child out your way to answer your complaint and catch you with your own hands in the cookie jar. The two of you make an awkward load for one packhorse and I ain't ready to head back to Meeker. So I reckon we'll have to do it cavalry field style."

Not wanting to spend the night close to even a fresh cadaver, he hauled Newt Harper out of his chosen campsite by the ankles, to wait alongside his victim, Tony, for a spell. There was no call to dig holes in the shallow soil around the outcrop. There were oodles of loose cobbles to be piled atop both bodies like short lengths of stone walling. He put young Tony's hat over the ruined horror of his face as he confided aloud, "He suspected I might be on to him before the two of you chased after me, old son. Once I confided I was fixing to catch up with the Menzies-MacAlpin sisters and, worse yet, *talk* to them, he knew he had to kill us both whilst he had the chance."

Tony didn't answer.

Longarm hadn't expected him to. As he gently placed a flat rock over the crown of the dead boy's hat Longarm muttered, "Now if only I had the least notion why that gal says a pair of hired guns were up this way after me! For I don't. It makes no sense! If old Newt yonder hired a couple of professionals to murder this child, why did he wait this long to try it his own fool self?"

Chapter 19

They got into Rock Springs on the Union Pacific line a little over forty-eight hours later, lathered some. There being no way in hell the sly MacAlpin sisters could have driven all those cows half that far in half that time, Longarm had plenty of time to get set up for their arrival, if he'd guessed right.

If he'd guessed wrong, he was up shit creek, with no idea what in hell was going on.

He wired the sheriff's department, down Meeker way, about the bodies he'd left for them to recover. To save them heaps of bother Longarm cheerfully confessed to gunning the late Newton Harper after the latter had murdered his own rider, Tony Mason, but said he was still working on Harper's motive for the crime. It felt dumb to have to backtrack and admit you'd been jumping to conclusions.

Knowing that whether he was guessing wrong or guessing right he was just about out of guesses, Longarm sold the trail-worn army stock at a minor profit, getting the taxpayer's money back with enough left over for a shave, a haircut, a steam bath and a fresh shirt and underwear, with bay rum thrown in.

Then he checked himself with his saddle and possibles into the Union Pacific Hotel across from the station of the same, and let folk get used to his face in their tiny town before he pushed his luck further.

He let a couple of trains pass through and pick up such stock as was on hand there before he ambled over to the stockyards, smiling, and offered a cheroot to both the young pokes he found roosting on a corral pole near the dispatcher's shed. He jawed about cows in general a spell before he casually said, "Last time I was up this way I was drinking with some old boys off that Hundred and Ten spread up the line. You ever hear tell of that outfit?"

One of the kids said, "Sure we have. Hundred and Ten Brand Cattle and Land, headquartered over to Thayer Junction. They buy and sell to fatten or ship. They're all right. Leastways, I've never heard anything bad about 'em."

Longarm mused, "Wonder what that hand was doing this far west, then."

The other hand said, "That's easy. They often ship out of these very yards. Like old Tom here says, they deal in beef, and beef prices are up back east, now that the railroad-scandal depression seems to be over. I've never visited their home spread, but the way I understand it they husband their breeding stock and buy the increase of others to ship, knowing the eastern market better."

The first hand confided, "Mayhaps in the biblical sense. They do say the Widow Menzies is a looker who drinks fizzy wine and eats fish eggs since she's been wined and dined in Omaha by big-shot buyers!"

Longarm just looked stern. The one called Tom suggested that was a dangerous way to talk about a lady with grown men riding for her.

Longarm changed the subject, asked if there was any other kind of action in Rock Springs, and when they both laughed at him, he mosied on to the dispatch shed. Figuring an old railroading man would not want to gossip about interstate commerce, Longarm produced his badge and warrant along with another cheroot. When the old-timer asked who they were after, Longarm turned a card over. The dispatcher told him the Hundred and Ten Brand Cattle and Land Company had indeed reserved holding pens and a loading chute out in the yards, with a view to shipping a whole lot of beef on the hoof within forty-eight hours.

So all Longarm had to do was wait, like a wise old tabby by a mouse hole when there wasn't a single gal running loose in Rock Springs as far as he ever determined.

Worse yet, it was the wrong time of the month for fresh reading material, save for copies of the *Rocky Mountain News* at the newstand in the lobby, printed two days earlier.

Reading the same in the shade of a paper palm tree, under an oil lamp that evening, Longarm was mildly surprised to learn a long-wanted paid assassin called Studs Bacon was languishing under police guard down in Denver General after he and what he described as a business associate called the Quicksilver Kid had shot it out with another loser known as Pat Tracy in the stairwell of a Denver office building.

Longarm didn't waste much worry time on a faraway local problem for Denver PD. He wasted time breaking even in a protracted penny-ante poker game with other hotel guests who didn't cheat. Poker games went on forever when nobody cheated.

But as in the case of that watched pot taking forever to boil, his slick maneuver paid off the following night, after a windless sunny day that lasted over a million years.

The Hundred and Ten Brand riders had maneuvered mighty slick as well. They'd grazed those two hundred head south of the tracks all afternoon to drift them in slow in the dusty gloaming light of a long mountain sunset. As Longarm watched from a hotel window, instead of right next to a mouse hole, he couldn't make out the brands, and most of the dozen odd riders sat their nondescript ponies as blurs. Longarm only made out the point rider as likely Una MacAlpin because she rode sidesaddle with no hat.

Longarm stayed put, smoking a cheroot with his rump on the windowsill as he gave them time to settle in over to the railroad yards. He had to account for the other sister, Elsbeth Menzies nee MacAlpin, ere he moved in to settle accounts.

But they didn't give him the time to move in smooth. He barely made it over to the yards in time when he guessed what that fast approaching train whistle might mean.

When he got himself and his saddle over to the tracks, it already meant it. The eastbound night train was a passenger-freight combination. In this case practical considerations put the passenger section up closer to the coal-burning locomotive but ahead of the stinky cattle cars. They were loading the cattle aboard as Longarm flashed his I.D. to the conductor and his federal badge to the federal crew of the mail car. He was watching from the doorway of the same when Una Menzies got aboard with most of her riders. To that rustic kid perched on a corral pole, Thayer Junction was not worth the hard ride and hence outside human ken. It would have taken Longarm till close to midnight following the U.P. service road and Western Union poles in his saddle, but in point of fact the cross-country combination had barely started out of Rock Creek before it was slowing down for the next stop at Thayer Junction. The mail crew warned him they wouldn't be there long. He stood near the open door with his saddle until he saw Una MacAlpin's sidesaddled palomino being led off into the dark. He dropped off to follow it, glancing idly back toward the cattle cars to the rear. Then the train started up with a metallic snap of its long spine and Longarm spun to run after it, moaning, "Suckered again!"

He saw it was no use and tagged along after the hand leading Una's palomino on foot. They had to be going somewheres, even if the owner was on her way to Omaha with all those cows off the N Circle H, and there were other ways to skin the same cat.

Longarm wasn't surprised when the hand leading Una's palomino and another pony led the boss lady's mount into a livery stable on Center Street before riding off faster than Longarm could follow on two booted feet, bless his heart.

Longarm had been through the junction before, so, knowing any gals who did business there would know the place better, he toted his load to a Chinee chop suey joint he knew of old, enjoyed a set-down supper of those noodles and foo eggs Chinee prefered to chop suey, and after they remembered him he asked if he could leave his McClellan and Winchester in their care.

They said they'd hide his gear and fight beside him. For nearby Rock Springs was a coal mining town mostly owned by the railroad. When the white miners had struck for higher wages back in '75, the U.P. brought in Chinee railroad builders to dig coal for them cheaper. Fair was fair, and it hadn't been the ambition of the Sons of Han to work their asses off for coolie wages. So word had gotten around in many a Chinatown across the West about a firm but fair white lawman who'd been as straight with both sides during the Chinee Riots of the seventies.

Once he was shed of his awkward baggage, Longarm legged it over to the offices and town house of the Hundred and Ten Brand Cattle and Land Company. He knew he'd given the sister he was hoping for time to settle in after her kid sister had slickered him. She was alone upstairs when he climbed the outside steps of her frame office building and knocked. He knew she had to be the older sister when she owned up to being the Widow Menzies. But she didn't look more than twenty-five or so. After that her hair was naturally auburn and hung down wavier than her kid sister's. It was hanging down for the night because she was dressed for retiring, in a green velveteen kimono and sheer ecru nightgown. Longarm could tell it was sheer because her kimono hung open a mite.

He introduced himself up front, and honestly, figuring it was time somebody commenced to level with somebody.

She said, "Come in. I've been expecting you, albeit not at this hour. Our mutual friend, Kim Stover, closer to the South Pass, told me you'd been asking about my sister, me and our brand."

As he followed her into a well-appointed, cozy setting room, Longarm removed his hat, muttering, "I heard the three fastest means of communicating were telegraph, telephone and tell-a-woman. What did old Kim tell you about me? I was hoping when I didn't tell her not to tell you she might not tell you."

The auburn-haired Elsbeth waved him to a seat, on a divan covered with a darker shade of green plush, and coyly remarked, "I don't know you well enough yet, to repeat her warnings to me about you in detail. You prefer Maryland rye to our malt liquor, right?"

Longarm said, "I'll drink most anything wet but turpentine, ma'am. I don't mind Scotch whiskey if it's mixed with a little branch water. I understand your young sister, Miss Una, went to Omaha on business?"

Elsbeth stood with her curvaceous back to Longarm as she fixed them some ice breakers at room temperature, saying, "Delivering a shipment of beef in person. Sometimes, when your road brands confuse buyers, it's reassuring to them when they finalize the sale with someone they know personally. Kim Stover said you seemed interested in our brand . . . ?"

As she handed him his highball and sank down close beside him, he told her, "Not no more. When I wired Miss Kim it had just occurred to me how the smaller One-Ten could be run to a bigger-looking N or H without much trouble. Extend the first two digits with a slanty crossbar and two more on the far side cross connected to make an H, and danged if we ain't got the late Newt Harper's Colorado brand!"

She blinked and asked, "Did you say the *late* Newt Harper?"

He said, "I shot him. I had to. He was fixing to shoot me."

She dropped her drink on the rug to throw both arms around him and kiss him on the mouth in a far from sisterly way.

Longarm kissed back as any man would have, managing with effort not to spill his own highball, but when they came up for air he sternly said, "Hold on! My boss warned me you'd try to seduct me so's I'd be bashful about arresting you. So before you seduct me a lick further I'd better tell you what I have on you and your sister."

She snuggled closer to protest, "We haven't done anything wrong. Not *really* wrong, when you study on it!"

Longarm said, "Let's study on it. The Hundred and Ten Brand Cattle and Land Company sold the late Newt Harper the seed stock for his own Colorado herd up here in Wyoming. We're talking a pretty penny if you gave him a price on scrub stock."

She said, "We surely did. His dear old wife had been kindly when my husband died. We sold Newt two thousand head at five dollars a head. Then he deserted his dear old wife and drove 'em south by way of the Flaming Gorges and canyonlands of the Yampa, whilst we tried to figure out where they were. His wife went back to her kin in Omaha, where the two of them hailed from, and if you ask me she was well rid of him before you shot him. I can't wait to tell her. She'll be so pleased!"

Longarm said, "Whatever sort of husband he was, Newt Harper got his new herd safely down to Rio Blanco County, where he already had a homestead claim along the White River and a beef contract with the federal government. But as a paid-up member of the wives union, you were at feud with him, and having sold him all that beef as you just confessed, you and your kid sister determined to steal it back from him. You knew you'd be logical suspects. So you wanted it *known* he'd been robbed by unseen hands riding with *other women*. You took turns letting yourselves be described, not the way you usually appear up here in Wyoming, and took advantage of modern science to make it seem impossible those outlaw gals could be you two."

Sipping his Scotch highball to wash the taste of her breath mints away, he continued, "We're only the second generation exposed to the iron horse and singing wire. So lots of folk still think in terms of moving cross-country ahorse or afoot, losing sight of the duck soup simple fact a man could murder his wife in Frisco and be entertaining an alibi housewarming in New York within the same week. Knowing you only needed one juror to buy your razzle-dazzle of maintaining that office downstairs during business hours whilst one or the other of you stole cows less than a week's drive south of your other outlet at Rock Springs—"

The auburn-haired widow woman put a hand on Longarm's thigh to cut in, "Custis, the check bounced. We let him have those cattle at a more than fair price and our bank sent his check back, marked insufficient funds. When we wrote him about it, he never answered. When we asked our lawyer, he said we couldn't charge him with criminal fraud for being overdrawn on a legitimate account. He said we had to sue him in Rio Blanco County if we couldn't get him to come back to Wyoming, and with the current price of beef at an all-time high, we just didn't have the time! So we decided it would be simpler to just take our cows back."

Longarm asked, "Do you still have the bounced check?"

When she said she did, he shook his head wearily and said, "You went about it all wrong and sure caused everyone else a heap of bother. But when you combine documentation of a bad debt with Newt Harper shooting one of his own riders and trying to shoot me before we could ever have this talk, I fear no jury in the land would hand you more than a good scolding. So there's just no sense in my arresting you."

Elsbeth giggled girlishly and asked if that meant she got to seduce him after all.

To which Longarm could only reply as he took her in his arms, "I thought you would never ask!"

So a few minutes later, right after Longarm had determined she had auburn hair all over, it was Elsbeth Menzies nee MacAlpin, a bad girl of Rio Blanco, who got to gleep, "Oh, my God, Kim Stover never warned me about *this,* you big moose!"

Chapter 20

Thinking back on the way bigger rump of good old Marlene Keller down in Meeker, Longarm found it a whirling wonder that two white women could be built so different and still have so much to offer. Elsbeth intimated she found *him* a new experience as they went at it hammer and tongs in a familiar position that felt forever fresh when you were doing it with somebody new. She didn't insult his intelligence by telling him she hadn't been getting any lately. She just acted like she hadn't. He felt no call to brag about any of *his* recent adventures either. But of course, once they'd come, three ways, and took time to share a smoke and a cuddle, propped up against the head of her bed in the next room, Elsbeth wanted to hear more about his adventures down in Colorado, chasing her kid sister whilst she minded the store up Wyoming way.

She thought it amusing how young Una had slickered him out on the open range that day, sidesaddle, until he explained how Una had slipped up twice, grabbing Scotch names and real brands out of thin air as she no doubt barely managed to keep from pissing her underpants, sidesaddle.

He said, "I'd have caught up with you pretty little

sneaks a whole lot sooner if it hadn't been for extra pieces of the puzzle I am still working on."

She asked how he could possibly think at this late date she was still holding *anything* back from him.

He kissed the part of her hair and said, "I never said you nor Miss Una gave orders to kill me before you could have known I was on my way to cut your sign. We've established you didn't even try for old Newt Harper's scalp after he'd swindled you so cruel."

She suggested, "Maybe *he* ordered you killed, before he tried to kill you, himself, I mean."

Longarm shook his head and said, "Won't work. More than one reason. To begin with old Newt *sent* for me, or somebody like me. Had he been worried about me seeing through his two faces earlier, he could have saved himself the bother by never sending for me."

"But once you started to get warm . . . ," she tried.

Longarm said, "I had this feeling there were others in the game all along. But nobody working for old Newt or you two sisters could have had orders to mess with me. Newt had to shoot his own Tony Mason for the simple reason young Tony, like all his other hands, bought his two-faced tale he'd paid honest money for the cows they were herding for him. Everyone riding for the N Circle H struck me as straight-shooting hands, save for their boss himself."

He took a drag on their shared cheroot and added, "I'll allow I was *starting* to wonder about frayed edges to his tale of woe, but had he not confessed right out by trying to kill me before we could have this conversation, we might never have had such a friendly conversation. So I fear those loose ends still fretting me must be a tedious example of the Poker Player's Paradox."

"The poker players *what*?" she asked, twisting some hairs south of his belly button.

He replied, "A paradox is when two statements each make the other impossible. For example, these two poker players go into this card house one Saturday night, feeling lucky. So they each ante up for exactly one dozen deals before they both quit whilst they are ahead and call it a night. Each one brags he lost four hands but won eight times. Neither poker player is lying and no games that night ended in a draw. Your turn."

Elsbeth no doubt prided herself on adding and subtracting figures, and the arithmetic was simple. It only took her moments, letting go his pubic hairs to count on her fingers, before she declared in a certain tone, "It just won't add up to two truthful tales, Custis! Nobody at their table, no matter how many there might have been, could be dealt twelve hands and win eight times without all the others he was playing with *losing* more than the four times one or the other had to be bragging about!"

Longarm told her, "I just said neither player was lying. They both played a dozen hands to lose four and win eight. Add it up."

She said something in the Gaelic that sounded dirty and insisted, "I have! More than once! What's the catch, Custis? There has to be a catch, right?"

He cuddled her closer and said, "Sure there is. But you can wrestle with it in vain forever if you figure they're bucking *one another*. I said these two poker players go into this card house one Saturday night feeling lucky. I never told you they sat down to play at the *same table* in the *same game,* did I?"

Elsbeth laughed like hell, grabbed him by his old organ grinder and vowed she'd make him pay for that.

Yet somehow it didn't hurt at all.

Next morning, serving him jam on buttered toast in bed, with the sunlight through the blinds painting tiger stripes across her swell tits and belly, down to her auburn thatch, Elsbeth brought up that Poker Player's Paradox again. Women never seemed to stop thinking, even when they were giving French lessons. A man had to watch what he said in moments of passion lest it come back and hit him at the damndest times.

Elsbeth asked if Longarm had any notion who the third and possibly more sinister player in their poker game might have been.

Washing down some toast with the tea she served instead of coffee, being Scotch, Longarm said, "Ain't dead certain how many players might have been at the table with us, if any were there at all. It's *possible* I ran into sinister strangers just because they had to be *somewheres* as I was passing through. But after a magical gal who has to be up to *something* sniffs all around you, and paid assassins working out of Denver shoot it out with others you *know* were after you, it gets sort of confounding."

"Then you'll be up this way awhile, wrapping up the case?" she asked him, hopefully.

Longarm patted her rounded rump fondly with his free hand as he witfully asked, "What case? Your kid sister fibbed to me? I'd look like a moon calf if I waited till she got back from Omaha and tried in vain to hang an obstruction charge on her. Like I said, you only need one juror who'd say you sisters had the right to repossess your unpaid-for cattle, however informally, to get off laughing at us. So I reckon I'll have to get it on down the railroad tracks to Denver. I can change to a southbound at Cheyenne. That's how come I got shed of two good old army broncs."

She asked if he could at least stay over the weekend. He knew he could get away with that, the office being closed in any case, but as they parted in the cold gray light of Monday morn it was all he could do to keep her from traveling at least as far as Cheyenne with him.

But Cheyenne was another story. *Her* name was Beverly and she slung hash in the U.P. dining room, and then it was on to Denver of a bright and sunny Wednesday afternoon, where Billy Vail declared in his smoke-filled office it was about time.

Vail said, "I got your wire from Thayer Junction days ago, even if you did send it night letter rates. Did you stray up to the South Pass to console that Widow Stover some more, you infernal Romeo?"

Longarm replied with a clear conscience, "You have my word I never laid eyes on Kim Stover, this trip. As a matter of fact I'm kind of vexed with old Kim. She might be holding a grudge about a sort of fuss we had the last time we met up back east. She might have caused me some trouble by tipping off another member of her union I'd been asking questions. But in the end it all turned out just swell. So what the hell."

"You never told me you'd met up with that rich Widow Stover on one of your missions farther east," Vail observed with a dirty grin.

Longarm observed he never told such tattletales, and since this was true, he had no call to go into that screaming fit old Kim had thrown when he'd gently but firmly refused to let her make a rich as well as honest man out of him.

He said, "Like I told you in that night letter, Newton Harper was a bigger crook than the young businesswomen he'd bilked out of ten thousand dollars with a bum check. The sheriff's department and their coroner's office over to Rio Blanco County are satisfied justice has been done. They wired me care of Cheyenne, like I told 'em. They were sorry I'd put my own bullet so close to Newt's ticker, once they went up to recover the bodies and discovered how messed up poor Tony Mason was. The rightful owners of the beef Harper bought with a bum check got a good part of it back, and with beef prices going through the roof they've more than made up their loss by reselling the cows they got back for forty bucks a head in Omaha, less shipping."

"You say the sassy sister acting as a decoy on that palomino as she flirted her way right past you was in Omaha whilst you were up Wyoming way, wrapping up the loose ends?" asked Billy Vail with one bushy eyebrow arched.

Longarm innocently replied, "So they told me. Had to take their word she wasn't in Thayer Junction, 'cause I never saw her there."

"Who'd you talk to about the pretty little thing up yonder?" his boss inquired with less interest as he worked at getting one of his awful stogies going again.

Longarm said, "Older woman working in their office. Those cigars wouldn't go out on you like that if you didn't keep them so soggy in that humidor, Billy."

Vail said, "A lot you know about good cigars. The dry climate of this mile-high city makes it imperative to keep fine tobacco from drying out. That's what they call storing 'em with plenty of water in your humidor, imperative. They tried to keep that hired gun you wired about from drying out, over to Denver General. But he died on you, night before last. Never confessed to shit. Even though Denver P.D. found him bleeding on the street just outside the stairwell where two other known gunslicks lay bleeding on the steps."

Longarm said, "I read about it in the *Rocky Mountain News.* Brung it to your attention because one of the dead on the stairs inside had lost a brother or a sidekick shooting it out with a hill tribe up in Glenwood Springs whilst I was there, albeit at another address."

"Was she pretty?" asked Vail, dryly.

Having no call to mean-mouth Miss Red Robin to a man she'd never done wrong, Longarm said, "That ain't the point. The point is that the so-called Tracy Twins, Pat and Mike, were in town, spoiling for a big shoot-out, and I suspect the one they got into must have been unplanned, because the surly assholes they shot it out with were out to shoot *me*! How do you like it so far?"

Old Billy Vail prided himself on how good he'd gotten at cutting sign along the paper trails from behind a desk since his younger and slimmer ranger days. So he beamed at Longarm with the smoldering stogie gripped in his grin, not a pretty sight, and declared, "What you read in last week's papers was old news. It's true that at first it seemed more mysterious to Denver P.D. For as you first read, they had what seemed a simple if deadly shoot-out betwixt known killers. Pat Tracy's lead was dug out of both Studs Bacon and the Quicksilver Kid. They figure it was Studs Bacon's lead they dug out of Pat Tracy. The shooting had taken place in a shabby business block near the municipal court and county jail. The steps led up to a paid-up member of the local courthouse gang. A lawyer Morrison, Jethrow Lowell Esquire. Are you getting warm?"

Longarm brightened and said, "Wasn't Lawyer Morrison the defense and business partner of that . . . let's see, Wagner, we put away on a federal mine claiming fraud?"

Billy Vail said, "He was. Wagner was his cousin as well as the front for Morrison's holding company. They had to let us put Wagner away to keep from going *with* him. I doubt they liked it much, and so when the copper badges first responded to the dulcet sounds of three six-guns singing in chorus, they naturally canvassed the building to make sure nobody else was hurt. Lawyer Morrison's office was at the head of those same stairs. But when they asked, the copper badges were told Lawyer Morrison had said something about visiting some mining property down the Front Range a piece. So they made sure his office door hadn't been forced and put the shooting down to personal spite having nothing to do with anyone in the building. Most gents on the prod for a killer like Pat Tracy would be inclined to fight it out with him in a dark stairwell rather than out in public."

Longarm said, "Pat Tracy sure was busy with his little six-gun. But have you any notion why he was down *here* shooting it just after another big shoot-out up in Glenwood Springs?"

Vail grinned like a kid swiping apples off a pushcart and said, "Ain't stuck with no *notion*. I *know* what happened! Few days after the unsettlement on the stairs, with Studs Bacon refusing to say a word, other tenants of that building commenced to suspect that something was rotten in Denmark, or in this case downtown Denver. So they forced the door of Lawyer Morrison, and guess what they found inside, lying in a Murphy bed he kept for working late or entertaining lady clients?"

Longarm whistled and asked, "That crooked lawyer himself?"

Vail said, "With a lady client called Madame Fatima. Some sort of vaudeville fortune-teller. Both bare-ass and over-ripe. Denver P.D. Homicide figures Pat Tracy killed them both, then ran into Bacon and the Quicksilver Kid on his way out. The three of them were known to work as hired guns for Morrison. Try her this way. Morrison sent them Tracy Twins after you, and when they tangled with those other pals of yours so fatally, Pat added one and one to get three. End of the story with all the loose ends tied up!"

Longarm exclaimed, "The hell you say! Slickers like Lawyer Morrison don't go in for belated revenge for no good reason!"

Vail smugly replied, "He thought he *had* a good reason when he heard we were sending you up to Rio Blanco County. You'd played a small but important part in convicting his cousin on a mineral claims fraud down in the Trinidad *coal fields*. Leopards seldom change their spots and guess who's been selling *coal futures stock* based on unproven coal claims up around Rangely, Rio Blanco County? Ain't it a bitch what a guilty conscience can do to a slicker you'd expect to be smarter?"

"You're right," said Longarm cheerfully. "End of the story with all the loose ends tied up!"